To Robbi,

In love & letters.

Jack N

This one's for Katie.
Always Love.

Wha

Never

Zach

t We

Had

Wyner

A Genuine Vireo Book | Rare B

Wha

Neve

Zach

Books

Publisher's Cataloging-in-Publication data

Names: Wyner, Zach, author.
Title: What we never had : a novel / by Zach Wyner.
Description: First Trade Paperback Original Edition. | New York, NY ; Los
Angeles, CA: Rare Bird Books, 2016.
Identifiers: ISBN 978-1-942600-68-8
Subjects: LCSH Bildungsromans. | Friendship—Fiction. | Dating (Social
customs)—Fiction. | Man-woman relationships—Fiction. | BISAC FICTION/
General.
Classification: LCC PS3623.Y646 W43 2016 | DDC [Fic]—dc23

"We consume ourselves in the beloved woman, we consume ourselves in the idea we believe, we burn in the landscape we are moved by."

—Milan Kundera, *The Book of Laughter and Forgetting*

Y OU SAT AT ONE of three study-room tables in The Homework Club with Adrienne, a fifteen-year-old recently-gone-goth student of yours with green hair, bad skin, and zero patience for stupidity. She was the last student left and was deeply absorbed in *The Great Gatsby*. For five hours, a steady trickle of teenagers had come and had gone—agitated, medicated, hormonal vessels of their parents' projected insecurities. Now it was cool and quiet. Just you, Adrienne, the stuffed bookshelves, and trace scents of Axe Body Spray and bubble gum. You yawned decadently, leaned back in your seat and stared at the periodic table of elements tacked to the wall. Every minute or so a turning book page cut through the hum of the air conditioner.

"Josh?"

"What's up, Aid?"

She rolled her eyes.

"Drienne," you said. "Adrienne."

She dog-eared the page she'd been reading. "My English teacher said that this is a *perfect* book."

Your cell phone rang. You took it out of your pocket and glanced down: June, calling for the first time in just over three months. A moth in your belly beat its wings.

"You all right?"

"Huh?" You shut the phone off and stuffed it deep inside your pocket. "Of course. Why?"

"Your face. You just looked like me when I get a geometry test back."

"I'm fine," you said, trying not to sound defensive. She looked down at her book. You followed her gaze to the cover of *Gatsby*—an indelible pair of eyes, irises transformed into reclining female nudes. "'Perfect,' eh?"

"Huh?"

"Your teacher. *Gatsby.*"

"Right."

"Maybe, for your teacher, it perfectly demonstrates the myth of the American dream. Maybe that's what he meant."

She scrunched her eyebrows together. "Why do you assume that my English teacher is a he?"

You smiled, no comment safe from her scrutiny. "I don't."

"You said 'maybe that's what *he* meant.'"

You shrugged. "Why would I assume that your teacher is a he?"

"I don't know. That's what I was…" She squinted suspiciously. "You're trying to confuse me."

You put up your hands, palms out. "I don't know what you're talking about, Aid."

She frowned.

"Drienne. Adrienne."

"When was the last time you read this?"

"I don't know. Eleventh grade?"

"What, like twenty years ago?"

You made a face, rolled your eyes. If she'd been two years older you would've given her the finger or made a comment about her hair, but Adrienne was a bit fragile, the type of kid who held her breath after doling out an insult.

"Look," you said. "I don't want to knock your teacher, but 'perfect' is kind of a ridiculous thing to say about any work of art."

"Right!" she said. "It's completely subjective."

"It's kind of like he's implying that there's something wrong with you if you don't get as much out of it as he does."

"That's what I… Wait! You did it again! You said 'he'!"

You waved your hand dismissively.

"You did!"

You sighed. "Well he is, isn't he?"

"Well…yeah."

"Your English teacher's 'perfect' book isn't *The Bluest Eye*, right?"

"Not everyone fits those kind of stereotypes, Josh."

"You're right. Not everyone does. But not everyone doesn't, either. A tenth grade English teacher whose perfect book is *Gatsby*? I'd go with male, between forty and fifty years old, on the scruffy side, lots of beige clothing."

"And you'd be wrong because he wears mostly denim."

You chuckled and scratched your prematurely thinning hair. "My point is that people only declare a piece of art to be perfect if they're trying to prove something. That statement sounds to me like a kind of justification. And women don't do that, at least not female high school teachers. They tend to be too secure to use words like 'perfect' when the topic of discussion is, as you said, something as subjective as literature."

Adrienne chewed her lip. The air conditioning switched off and in the new quiet, the whine of the florescent lights was audible.

"I can never tell when you're being serious."

"I'm always serious."

She snorted. "Yeah. And I'm a cheerleader."

You laughed. Adrienne smiled victoriously and returned to her reading.

You were one of three study room tutors at The Homework Club, there to serve all non-private students who came in search of the three S's: Support, Structure, and Studiousness. You took your job seriously. You had to. It was 2003, eight years since you'd graduated high school, and it wasn't as though you'd mastered the material the first time around. You'd been a good student. The kind of student who got mostly Bs and who was somewhat justified in claiming to your college friends that you could have gotten mostly As if you'd really applied yourself, if that's where your priorities had been. But you didn't have any real priorities in high school—not beyond drinking beer, playing music with your buddies, and pining for Rachel Schwartzman and her superior tits. You'd realized that people had ideas about you, about what you should be wanting and how you should be going about getting it, so you did just enough to mollify them, to relegate their expectations, to demonstrate that you were going to work at your own pace. You put energy into friendships, acting, and music; you didn't have the kind of reserves that would allow you to put the same energy into chemistry, too. Maybe that's why you remembered the time fondly.

Adrienne had priorities, too, but you weren't certain to whom they belonged. At this point in time, her primary focus seemed to be survival. Her parents used The Homework

Club like an extravagant babysitting service, instructing their chauffeur to drop her off after school and leave her there until the place shut down at nine. Adrienne filled those hours fluctuating between rage—litanies of injustices suffered at the hands of jocks, twits, and ineffectual teachers—despair—near tears over a math test she was certain to fail—and placid acceptance—reading, drawing comics, ordering take-out from the falafel place next door, painting her nails various shades of discontent, and counting the minutes until college.

"You get that Emerson essay back yet?" you asked.

She kept her eyes fixed on *Gatsby*. "I got an A."

You smacked the tabletop. "I told you. I freaking told you."

She smiled. "You told me that transcendentalism was a bunch of crap."

You chuckled.

"What?" she said.

"You're dangerous."

"Why?"

"Because you remember all the crap that comes out of my mouth."

Shortly after nine o'clock, the chauffeur pulled up to the curb outside and honked. Adrienne hefted her onerous backpack and headed for the door, bent at the waist like an Egyptian slave toting a stone up the pyramid steps.

"See you tomorrow?" you said.

"I'm leaving early tomorrow. I have animation class and violin."

"It's a busy life," you said.

"Tell me about it."

"Hey, Adrienne."

She stood in the open doorway. In rushed street noise, car exhaust, thick gusts of sticky September air.

"Nothing," you said. "Have a good night."

She squinted, suspicious of adult words that went unsaid. "Such a weirdo," she said, and left it at that. The door swung shut, returning you to the air-conditioner and the fluorescent lights, the whine and hum of your everyday.

*

YOU BYPASSED YOUR NORTH Hollywood apartment and drove straight for The Burrow. You felt somewhat guilty. You had houseguests, Bill and Amare, two friends who'd recently moved down to LA from Olympia, Washington, and had been crashing in your living/dining room for the past two weeks. What had been intended to be a stopgap was beginning to resemble permanence. They knew that the current arrangement— three guys in their mid-twenties, crammed into a junior one-bedroom apartment—was untenable, but knowledge was only half the battle. It was all a matter of inertia, and Bill and Amare at rest tended to stay at rest unless acted upon by an outside force. You were having a hard time exerting that force.

That didn't mean that you were going to go out of your way to invite them to a bar. Yes, they needed to get out of the apartment, and yes, you were having difficulty identifying where their asses ended and your couch began, but The Burrow wasn't the kind of place they needed to go. The Burrow was a recuperative environment for people with jobs, where drinks were stiff and the jukebox had an abundance of tunes that reached back further than Los Angeles' collective memory of two-to-three months. For the likes of Bill and Amare, guys who, on any given day, had nowhere in the world they needed to be,

The Burrow was a trap even more perilous than that television they'd planted themselves in front of two weeks ago.

You exited the freeway at Los Feliz Boulevard, squeezed into The Burrow's narrow, poorly lit parking lot and found Harrison James-Deaning against the red brick exterior wall. Having fled his parents' Inland Empire home and his job as a substitute teacher a week ago, Harrison was renting a cheap, by-the-week motel room around the corner while he studied for the LSATs. Freshly shaven, he looked gaunt and ashen, as though it had been a while since he had seen the sun and/or consorted with a diurnal species. He nodded when he saw you and expelled twin jets of smoke from his nostrils. The fact that he didn't hug you indicated that he hadn't been there long, probably just long enough for a single round. Two whiskey and ginger ales from The Burrow had a way of ushering one abruptly into a state of physical affection.

"Hey," he said.

"You hanging in there?"

"I called you to cancel. Your phone went straight to voicemail."

You took your phone out of your pocket. You'd forgotten to turn it back on after the June call. "And yet here you stand."

Harrison pinched his cigarette between his thumb and forefinger and took a final drag. "I couldn't reach you. What choice did I have?" He dropped the cigarette and ground it into the asphalt with the sole of his shoe. The three-hundred-pound doorman with the words *Mama's Boy* tattooed on his neck stared at him. Harrison picked up the butt and tossed it in the ashtray.

You entered the dimly lit room, its row of stained glass windows near the ceiling keeping the street light at a comfortable remove; freshly popped popcorn masked the mildewy bar smell, so pungent during the daytime. You spotted a pair of vacant stools.

"So many haters," said Harrison.

"The doorman?"

"He can suck a bag of dicks."

"I wouldn't take it personally," you said.

"Of course you wouldn't. We're not talking about you. You work with children for chrissakes."

"Teenagers."

"Even worse."

You sat down and signaled Leanne, a five-foot, ninety-pound Vietnamese woman, who imparted warmth and kindness with her strong drinks but made little in the way of chitchat. You appreciated her circumspection. You disliked a chatty bartender who thought that years spent absorbing hard-luck tales and doomed-before-they-hatched stratagems made them qualified analysts.

"Nice to see you again," she said to Harrison. "You becoming my most best customer."

"Medicine please, nurse."

She smiled and planted a couple seven-parts whiskey, one-splash ginger ales on the bar. Harrison took a long drink and stared at his reflection in the mirror behind the liquor bottles. He had a well-earned reputation for rapid transformations so you let him be. Once adequately lubricated his mood would brighten. In the meantime, you had to do something about the state of your stomach. The smell of popcorn was inducing a sound akin to a bleating goat.

Harrison interrupted your internal debate—whether to fill up on popcorn or run next door to the Del Taco—with a clandestine elbow to your ribs. At the end of the bar two conspicuously attractive girls were sipping brimming liquid from martini glasses.

"Now there's the kind of distraction I could justify," he said.

You winced.

He stood up and gave your arm a little tug. "Come on. Take the stick out of your ass and come talk to the pretty girls."

"Let me at least get some popcorn in my stomach."

"Joshua."

"I'm really not in the proper headspace."

He tugged harder. "C'mon."

"Dude!" you said. "Can't you just sit down and talk to me for a minute?"

He studied your face and chewed his lip pensively, as if estimating the amount of time it would take for you to adequately unburden yourself and whether or not the girls would still be without suitors after this interval had elapsed.

"Sure." He sat down. "Shit. Of course we can talk." He took a sip of his drink, glanced at the girls out of the corner of his eye and put his hand on your shoulder. "You all right? Everything okay?"

"Fine. It's fine. They're cute...the girls. I get it."

"Forget about the girls," he said. "I could give a fuck about those girls. Tell me what's going on."

You sipped your drink. "You ever hear of a lancet liver fluke?"

"They make that with vodka or gin?"

"Ha ha."

"Go on."

"A lancet liver fluke is a parasite."

"Sure."

"It gets inside an ant and manipulates its nerves so that, at dusk, instead of returning to the ant hill with the colony, the ant climbs a blade of grass." You placed your drink on a bar napkin; beads of condensation tumbled down the sides of the glass, transforming the stiff paper into something delicate and easily torn. "Anyway, it screws with the ant's nerves because it wants to get back into its host, which is a cow."

"Right on," he said.

"So, the fluke compels the ant to climb a blade of grass at dusk and then clamp its jaws down on the blade. Then, when the cow, its desired host, goes for its morning graze, it eats the ant."

He stroked his gaunt cheeks. "And then it lives in the cow?"

"In its liver."

"Why does it leave the cow in the first place?"

"Because it lays its eggs in the cow's shit."

"That's wild."

You reached for your drinks at the same time and downed them like synchronized swimmers.

"I'm missing something," he said.

You shook your head. "I thought you were a sharp guy."

He laughed. "So did I."

"I'm the ant."

"Come again?"

"I'm the fucking ant, climbing the blade of grass." You ran a cigarette lengthwise between your upper lip and your nose and inhaled fresh tobacco. "June called tonight."

Harrison's eyebrows raised but he didn't say a word. You peered down into your glass and rattled the ice cubes.

"I didn't answer."

"No?"

"It's why my phone was turned off."

"Well that's a fucking relief."

You shrugged.

"She leave a message?"

"I don't know."

"Ah," said Harrison. "Then you're not the ant yet, man." He wagged his finger at you. "The message is the what-do-you-call-it."

"Lancet liver fluke."

"Right. June is the fucking cow."

"Just knowing that she called, that a message may be there." You pointed at your head. "I feel like she's in here already, leading me away from the ant hill, overriding my instincts to function as a member of the colony."

"I don't think ants have instincts. They're all about the pheromones."

"That's true." You chuckled. "Maybe that would have made a better analogy."

"It's okay. I like the what-do-you-call-it story." He put his hand on the back of your neck and massaged it. "But Josh, dude, if I were your lawyer, this would be about the time that I reminded you of the existence of some rather infamous legislation in this state, pertaining to repeat offenders."

He kept massaging; you squirmed a bit in your seat and signaled Leanne for a refill.

His hand moved to your shoulder and squeezed. "Right now you've got a bulls-eye on your chest. It doesn't mean that you're necessarily going to prison, but statistics suggest that the likelihood of your spending some time behind bars is much greater than mine."

"I can't go back there," you said.

Harrison sipped his fresh drink. Then he looked you in the eyes and said, "Change your phone number."

"That's it?"

"It's the obvious solution. If you don't want her to contact you, change your fucking phone number. It's both a practical and symbolic gesture. I'd say change your email address too, but you never check that anyway."

There was a lengthy pause. The girls at the end of the bar, who'd been pushing buttons on the electronic dartboard for a couple of minutes without success, threw up their exasperated arms and turned toward the booths, then the bar, in search of qualified assistance. "And hey, since I'm in a generous mood here, I'm gonna dole out one more piece of advice."

You chuckled. "You think I should talk to the pretty girls?"

"Man's gotta eat, man's gotta live," he said, mischief blazing in his eyes like those incandescent city lights on the *Gatsby* cover. "Leanne, darlin'. Can I get some change for your dartboard?"

Leanne placed two more whiskey gingers on the bar for which you tipped generously. You felt for a moment as though you were standing in that yellow wood on which two roads diverged.

"I'm a man," you said.

"Attaboy."

*

YOU LEFT THE BAR around midnight with a pretty girl named Julia's phone number and a borderline-legal blood alcohol level. You made it home and opened the front door of your apartment to the smell of dirty socks and Bill, supine on the carpet in front of the television, both hands tucked behind his bald dome. Amare, sprawled on the couch like a listless house cat, lifted his head from the arm of the faux leather long enough to convey utter existential exhaustion before returning it to its resting place with a thud. The dining/living room area sagged under the weight of lowered expectations and a melatonin deficiency.

You put your keys and wallet on top of your bookshelf and stood next to the couch like an asshole, waiting for Amare to sit up and make room.

"The Sox blew it," said Bill. Fanatical Boston sports fans had raised both you and Bill. Given the circumstances, your shared allegiance to the Red Sox was at an all-time premium. "We're never beating the Yankees with this bullpen. Grady's trying out a new closer every fucking night. How are we supposed to make a playoff push when these guys don't know their roles?"

You stretched your arms above your head and yawned. "It's a valid concern."

Amare scratched his burgeoning potbelly. "The Sox bullpen is like the US Senate," he said. "The game gets turned over to them and they can't throw strikes. They just stall until the bed is officially crapped and your starters take no decisions."

"Anyway," said Bill, "They're on ESPN tomorrow. Last series of the season in the Bronx."

You fought the impulse to grab a beer from the fridge, succumb to lethargy and sink into the unoccupied cushion by Amare's pungent feet. You couldn't sit just yet. Even slightly buzzed you needed the contrast between his kind of weariness and yours to be clear, at least to you, at least for a few more minutes.

"You guys eat?" you said.

"Don't even mention food," said Bill.

Amare wagged a condemnatory finger at Bill. "Bubba Gump over here ate two orders of fried shrimp and chips."

"Ugh," groaned Bill. "Don't talk about it."

You stepped up into the designated bedroom area, a single-step and a curtain insinuating a separation between itself and the designated living room area. *Multi-level living*, you called it, a literal step up from a studio, but drawing that curtain was a daily reminder that you had yet to elevate yourself to the station in life that put plaster between you and your houseguests. You retreated to the bathroom and turned on the fan. The toilet seat was up. Thick droplets of yellow dehydrated piss sprinkled the rim of the bowl. The bath mat squished under your feet and water soaked through your socks. You peeled off your clothes and showered. You sucked down steam like it was vaporized Prozac. The hum of the ceiling fan obliterated the voices from the television and you remembered what it was like to be all alone—just you and a modest, clean, quiet multi-level room that the outside world was content to ignore.

For two weeks you'd been returning home, heavy-limbed and brain weary, from The Homework Club—following hours of helping teenagers with their geometric proofs and instructing them on the insipid art of the college application essay—only to find Bill and Amare in roughly the same positions as when you'd left. And yet, there was something about their lifestyle that you admired, something about their influence that you weren't so eager to jettison. The truth was that, up until a couple of weeks ago, you hadn't known them all that well—at least in terms of total hours logged. You'd met them a few years before on a trip up north to visit a group of high school buddies at Evergreen College. Throughout a week of drinking in dive bars and eating at greasy spoons, Bill and Amare had proven to be championship-caliber partiers, disappearing only to work the occasional shift at the Olympia Food Co-op or change their underwear. By week's end, bolstered by a foundation of laughter and communally nursed hangovers, your mutual love-at-first-wisecrack was cemented in eternal friendship. Those seven days might as well have been seven years. When the boys migrated to

Los Angeles and discovered their hostel was infested with rats, you'd been more than happy to offer shelter.

That first night, the three of you got drunk on whiskey, ordered take-out, and watched hours of reality television. Ordinarily, watching reality TV took you to a dark place; it sucked your life force, invigorated your latent cynicism. But watching *Temptation Island* and *Who Wants To Marry My Dad* with Bill and Amare produced the opposite feelings. It was cathartic and joyful; like a close brush with death, it reaffirmed just how alive you were. The next night, when you'd been tempted to do it all over again, it occurred to you that the line between you and your friends was not so clearly defined; it was a simple matter of resources and shame.

*

Sleep eluded you. Amare's deviated septum endowed his snoring with the unruly chortle of a diesel engine and Bill talked in his sleep in an eerily casual way, as if he were ordering dinner. You got up, pulled aside the curtain that separated the bedroom area from the living room area and observed their sprawled carcasses, marveling at their ability to sleep soundly under any circumstance. Your cigarettes accompanied you to the narrow balcony where you stood shirtless in eighty sultry degrees. Up above, tangled telephone lines buzzed like radioactive blood vessels, while, across the narrow alleyway, the blue light of insomniac television screens illuminated your neighbors' curtains.

You were getting to a certain age, one disconcertingly beyond the original age you'd set for yourself to quit smoking. A few years removed from college, you had a job that sounded serious enough to provoke approving nods from your elders, suggest that you didn't entirely lack ambition. But you'd taken the tutoring gig like you'd taken every other job before it—as a means to pay the bills while you worked on becoming whatever the fuck you were supposed to become. Ten months later, there was no denying that the job had taken its hammer and begun to chisel away superfluous pieces of rock, until what had once been an amorphous slab began to resemble something like an adult. And yet your habits set you firmly amongst a group of peers that other adults presumed you'd outgrown. The truth was, you didn't want to leave them behind any more than you wanted to leave behind your cigarettes. They were trusted companions. They made you happy. And they were brilliant. They were better at doing nothing than you'd ever been at anything.

You extinguished your cigarette in the giant ceramic ashtray that contained the butts of two, maybe three months. You rooted amongst them, pushing the pile this way and that until you got to the bottom and uncovered the fossil you'd been digging for: a lipstick-tipped Parliament. It was strange to think that not so long ago, June had been a constant in your life, a real person who left behind tangible proof of her existence, not just those psychic scars that, like a low-grade ringing in your ears, sank beneath the noise of the day only to resurface when all went dark and silent and still. There was a danger in talking about her like you had with Harrison, in creating analogies— it transformed her into an abstraction. The lipstick-tipped Parliament was a sobering reminder. Symbols don't smoke.

About six months after you and June had moved in together, she tried to organize a party for your twenty-fourth birthday. But, as so often happened when the two of you made plans requiring engagement with the outside world, tragedy struck in the form of botched reservation, an attempt by June to reschedule the whole affair, and your insistence that everything was cool, you should all just go for beers and burgers at that pub with the big patio on Sunset. Apparently, beers and burgers were not what June had in mind. Your cavalier attitude was also not what she had in mind. Transforming her unjustified, bad-news reputation by organizing a nice night out—this was what she had in mind. With this dream dashed, June locked herself in your bedroom and you sat in front of the television, nursing a glass of bourbon and chewing on a dilemma—if you went out and met up with your friends, June might be gone when you returned. According to her, there were any number of guys she could call who would drop whatever they were doing to come rescue her. Given the fact that you had once been one of those guys, you had no reason to doubt her. On the other hand, if you stayed, you'd lose face with your friends, and likely be forced to debase yourself with the kind of transparent lie that prompted people to avert their eyes for the duration of the telling. In the end you flaked on your friends and stayed home, wondering how many body blows your dignity could absorb and if this public acknowledgement of her power over you was the sort of push you needed to end it all.

The truth was that you'd never officially ended things. Your relationship with June was like the Korean War—left hanging. You'd leveraged a threat of eviction, made like it was as an opportunity. It wasn't a breakup, you'd said; it was a rewrite. Because you'd drafted it on loose scraps of paper, the story of the two of you had lost its thread. Sure, there might have been points in time when you could lay all the individual pieces out on the floor and recognize an architecture, but you lived in a goddamned wind tunnel, and daily your story was blown apart, reduced to a meaningless jumble of sentence fragments and disconnected words. At some point, tired of arranging and rearranging those disparate scraps, exhaustion won out.

Each of you needed to work on each of you before there could be any collective we. You needed a job; she needed her degree. And neither of those things were going to happen as long as you were both sleeping until two in the afternoon—sometimes later. Christ, there'd been more than a few dim winter days when you'd brewed your morning coffee just in time to watch the sunset. The thought still made you shudder.

This year you spent your birthday sans June and surrounded by friends. It was a joyous occasion filled with bonhomie and laughter and yet, at one late point in the evening, you were ambushed by the type of loneliness that preys upon unsuspecting birthday-boys in the midst of their most gregarious hour. In an instant, you knew that while you might have aged a year, you had not grown into the man whose self-respect would have demanded that he walk out on June's bullshit. Yes, you had physically separated, but the fact that a single phone call from her could trigger such distress suggested that you were still that same coward who had weaseled out on a technicality.

On your way back to bed, you accidentally kicked one of Bill's legs.

"Ow," he said in his sleep. "Sorry, Josh," he mumbled. "I'm sorry."

Your heart ached. You almost dropped to your knees and hugged him. Instead you went to the bathroom and rinsed ash from your hands. You brushed your teeth in the dark, switched the air conditioner to a lower, quieter setting and crawled back into bed.

*

It was the first week of September, the hottest week of the year in the San Fernando Valley. After slogging through traffic for an hour, you showed up early at The Homework Club and cooled off beneath a steady stream of conditioned air that frosted the quarter-sized bald spot on the top of your head. You studied an atlas, leafed through an algebra textbook and factored polynomials, pulled Howard Zinn off the shelf and read about the enslavement and slaughter of Indians that had taken place in California five hundred years before your arrival. Your gums, swollen from the morning's dental visit, a plaque-mining mission that your dental hygienist had referred to as "unusually bloody," throbbed as you sipped saccharine iced coffee from the Starbucks next door.

Your bosses, Tim Meeks and Eric Hubrisson, showed up just before 3:00 p.m. and disappeared into their shared office space. A few minutes later, Adrienne arrived, unburdened herself of her backpack, and sank into the nearest chair.

"Can I swear?" she asked.

"Permission granted."

"I fucking hate high school."

"Less than three years to go," you said. "You'll be outta there before you know it."

"I got a D on my geometry test. I'm going to be stuck in the tenth grade forever."

"It's one test, darlin'. Not the end of the world."

She moaned, leaned forward and thumped her forehead against the table. Her long, unruly green hair unraveled like yarn. You let her be.

At a quarter past four, the official commencement of study room hours, Sophie glided through the front door. A willowy seventeen-year-old backstroke champion with a gift for rendering even your most audacious male students mute, Sophie possessed a pair of eyes the precise shade of blue that caused oxygen to involuntarily evacuate lungs. She sat next to you, her damp hair still fragrant with post-swim-practice conditioner, and extricated from her backpack her notorious modeling portfolio. She opened it, planted it on the table between you and Adrienne, opened it and leaned back in her chair.

"Sophie!" said Adrienne. "Oh my god. I can totally see your…" Adrienne looked at you, covered her mouth, and blushed.

"What do you think, Josh?" said Sophie. "Too slutty?"

What could you do? Averting your eyes and thrusting your hands between you and the photo would only give her more power. So you looked. There, staring back at you like a couple plugs of red licorice behind a layer of sheer nylon, were Sophie's nipples. You took a moment, nodded, scratched your chin, faced her and fixed your gaze directly on those blue eyes.

"Soph," you said, "I think that you're more than a pretty face. I think that you're a good writer and that you should go to college someplace far far away from Los Angeles."

Sophie rolled her eyes and closed the book. "Whatever. That's such a Josh thing to say."

"She's right," said Adrienne. "That was very Josh."

You shrugged. What else were you supposed to tell her? The truth? That if you were seventeen, you would have given up smoking, rock and roll, and your driver's license to nail her? The truth was that Sophie was a crappy writer, but her level of crappiness was in no way exceptional. The vast majority of your students were crappy writers. Raised by a generation of parents who had convinced them that their every doodle was an impressionistic masterpiece, how could they be anything else?

"I like it, Sophie," said Adrienne. "You look real pretty."

"Yeah?"

"Duh."

"Thanks, Dri."

At five o'clock, Alexis and Caspian crashed through the door, faces flushed, their cell phones pressed their against their ears as avalanches of gossip fell from their mouths.

"No phones!" you said.

They rolled their eyes, dropped their bags in the middle of the room where they might inflict maximum damage on unsuspecting ankles, and headed back outside, their dialogues continuing unabated.

After an hour or so of actual study time, an assembly concerning boys, Sophie's modeling career, and the proper application of lip gloss formed in the rear of the study room. You went next door to *Pita Time!* and picked up shawarma wraps for Tim and Eric and a Greek salad for yourself. You returned to work, hefting a bulging, greasy sack, and four teenage heads turned as one.

"Hey, Josh," cooed Sophie. "How's June? We haven't seen her for a while."

"Who's June?" said another girl.

"Josh's girlfriend, duh."

A few months before summer vacation had started, June picked you up from work and a feeding frenzy had ensued: "Is Josh your boyfriend? Have you kissed him? Met his parents? Oh my god, have you slept over at his apartment? Does he correct your grammar? Does he try to talk about parabolas and subordinating conjunctions when you're on a date?" You were surprised to discover that these girls appeared to have never considered the reality of your social life. The Homework Club wasn't school. You weren't a teacher. You were young; you shared cultural reference points. You'd been certain that your fluency in *The Chapelle Show* and Cartoon Network's *Adult Swim* humanized you. But judging by their wide-eyed astonishment, it seemed that there was something about the role you played in their lives that was difficult to reconcile with a girlfriend.

"Give me a minute, girls," you said, heading for Tim and Eric's office.

"Josh is too busy for us."

"Josh has important things to do."

"Yeah. Like get Tim and Eric their dinners."

You closed your eyes. You inhaled deeply. You knocked on your bosses' door.

"Did you see that?"

"We made him mad."

"Josh is angry with us."

"Josh doesn't like us anymore."

You chuckled.

"Yay! Josh loves us!"

"Josh is totally in love with us."

The office door swung open. Tim and Eric, men in their early forties with potbellies, stress-wrinkled foreheads, graying hair, and impeccable SAT scores, reached for the food as if they'd been locked in there starving for days. Tim bit off a hunk of shawarma the size of your fist and handed you a five and what appeared to be six or seven crumpled ones.

"Keep the change," he said through a mouthful of tahini-smothered lamb.

The wraps were eight bucks apiece. It didn't take a perfect math score on your SAT's to calculate that you'd been hosed.

"Hey, Josh," said Eric, his eyes averted as he busied himself with the meticulous task of peeling back the tin foil from his wrap. "Sophie show you any pictures today?" He took a bite and stared into the wrap's glistening innards as he chewed.

You sighed. "The portfolio made an appearance. I tried to defuse the situation."

Eric put his food on the desk, pushed his glasses up the bridge of his nose and made eye contact. He liberated his ponytail from the collar of his shirt.

"I need you to not look at those pictures, okay?"

"Okay," you said, your belly beginning to tingle. "It's not as if I asked to see them."

Tim interjected, his mouth full. "Kevin's dad complained." He held up his index finger while he chewed his food and swallowed. "He said he overheard Kevin on the phone, telling his friend that a girl who studied here showed him naked pictures of herself."

"Okay," you said.

"I realize this may be somewhat awkward," said Eric, raising his eyebrows and looking at Tim.

"No," you said. "Wait. You realize what is awkward?"

"Just don't look at the pictures anymore, okay Josh?"

Electric currents radiated from your gut and shot through your appendages. You clenched your fists. You couldn't argue. Getting defensive would only make you sound guilty of whatever Eric was implying.

"What would you like me to do next time?"

"You know what?" he said. "Never mind. Maybe I better tell her myself to leave the portfolio at home."

You stood there a moment. He took another massive bite of shawarma. You waited a few beats. "You mean later?" you said.

He swallowed. "Obviously."

"Because she's out there right now."

"Well, I can't talk to her while I'm eating, can I?"

He punctuated the t in "talk" and a small piece of gnarled lamb rocketed from his mouth and landed on the floor. He pretended not to notice, turned back to his desk and shuffled paperwork.

"Thanks for getting the food, Josh," said Tim. "One of us will talk to her before she leaves."

You nodded in agreement and bolted before suggesting what they might do with their shawarmas.

There were times when it was clear that students were finished studying, when efforts made to keep them on track would result only in you doing their work for them. You walked out of Tim and Eric's office and recognized that Sophie and co. had crossed this threshold. With only a few minutes left of their study block, you succumbed to their chattiness and let the inevitable interrogation commence. The truth was, you were self-absorbed. When your students showed interest in your life, you divulged. It's up to every authority figure to draw a line in the sand, preserve their privacy. Your line could not withstand your desire to share. You regaled them with life experiences—nothing R rated, but definitely some PG-13 material. You did it because it made your students like you; you did it because sometimes, in a setting like The Homework Club, where maintaining order wasn't such a struggle, being liked was useful; you did it because you couldn't help yourself. Your life fascinated you. It seemed only natural that others might be fascinated by it as well.

Eric never emerged that night to talk to Sophie. He and Tim received their private students in the seclusion of their office and let you deal with the study room. At 6:30, Sophie's mom pulled up to the curb and honked. You broke off from the rest of the girls and followed Sophie to the door.

"Aw. You gonna open the door for me, Josh? What a gentleman."

"Look, Soph," you said. "I gotta say something before you go."

Sophie peered through the glass door and signaled to her mom to wait. She readjusted her grip on the portfolio. You knew that you didn't need to do this, but you thought that it might make you feel older somehow. This was about power after all and you'd had enough of it being wielded over you by both your bosses and your students.

You pointed. "It's about this."

Sophie looked down. She smiled coyly. "What about it?"

"I think that it might be best if you left it in your bag from now on."

She frowned, shifted her weight. She looked out the window at her mom's car. Then she looked back at you.

"Why?" she said. Her blue eyes flashed; your pulse quickened.

"It's becoming a distraction."

"Oh," she said. She lowered her head. You fought an impulse to give her a paternal pat on the back. "But talking about your ex-girlfriend isn't a distraction?"

"Excuse me?"

She raised her head and sneered. "How is talking about June for an hour not a distraction?"

"Whoa, whoa, whoa. First of all, Sophie, that was fifteen minutes, not an hour. And secondly, you *asked* me about June. I just answered questions."

"And Caspian *asked* me to bring my portfolio."

"It's not the...look. Sophie." All of a sudden you had a tremendous craving for a cigarette. "I don't think that those pictures are appropriate for the study room, okay?"

"Not appropriate?"

"They're good pictures, and they look really professional and all, but they're a little risqué. Don't you think?"

"Risqué?"

"Revealing. Too much so for this crowd."

Her mom honked twice. Sophie hiked her backpack and adjusted her grip on the portfolio.

"Look, Josh. My mom's waiting. I really gotta go."

You put your hand on the door to prevent her from leaving. She took a step backwards and her eyes widened as though you'd touched her as opposed to the door.

"Just promise me you'll leave the photos at home from now on."

"Josh!" she said. "I really need to go." Water flooded her blue eyes.

"Sophie," you pleaded.

"Please!"

You took your hand off the door and she charged outside, clutching her portfolio to her chest. The little bell affixed to the doorframe jingled meekly. She climbed into the back seat of her mother's SUV. You prayed the tears had just been a warning, that she wasn't sobbing to her mother about what a horrible person you were and how she was never going back to that awful place.

"What was that all about?" called a voice from the back of the room.

"What's wrong with Sophie?" said another.

"Nothing," you said. "Get to work."

"What's he talking about?"

"Work!" you said. "Homework! The thing you come here to do! The thing I get paid to help you with!"

They made faces that indicated they smelled something rotten or you'd sprouted a second head. You sat down in the nearest chair and took a series of deep breaths. The room was quiet except for their whispering, but you made no attempt to hear what they were saying. You could imagine its content well enough.

*

YOU ENTERED YOUR APARTMENT bearing gifts—a large pepperoni pizza and a twelve pack—and noted an atmospheric shift: the distinct absence of foot funk, the burnt hair scent of your vacuum's tired motor, and the citrusy scent of laundry detergent. You switched on the lights. The trash had been emptied, the recycling cleared out; grooves in the carpet betrayed the vacuum cleaner's path around the table and chairs. Overstuffed bags, presumably containing Bill and Amare's freshly laundered clothing, were tucked in the corner of the room. You didn't know what to make of it. You thought back to the only other time in the past two weeks that you'd returned home to find the apartment empty. There'd been an arcane note on the dining/living room table that read, *Off to see the Wizard.* You couldn't imagine a visit with a wizard taking less than a couple of hours, but you hadn't even had the time to drop your drawers and tug one out before they'd returned with microwave burritos and French Roast coffee from 7-Eleven. When you'd inquired about the note, Amare had looked at you curiously.

"You don't know Ozzie?"

"Ozzie."

"He lives at the 7-Eleven around the corner."

"I didn't realize they were leasing."

"The Wizard stands in front of the monitor every night for a couple of hours playing Super Lotto. One night Bill bet him ten bucks he couldn't eat two bacon cheeseburger dogs without yakking."

"What do you mean he stands there for a couple of hours?"

"It's Super Lotto Hot Spot."

"New draws every four minutes!" said Bill in his best approximation of a radio broadcaster.

"And…" You paused. "Did he do it?"

"Do what?" said Bill.

"Eat the dogs."

Amare smiled. "The Wizard can't refuse a wager."

"Did he yak?"

"Of course not. Dude's not called 'Wizard' for nothing."

You dropped the pepperoni pizza on the dining/living room table, cracked a beer, and ventured onto your balcony. Minus the boys and their detritus, your junior one-bedroom felt suddenly expansive. You had the curious realization that the amount of personal space that you required was diminishing by the day. You had expected the opposite would be true.

Growing up, your bedroom was your refuge, but it was not a sovereign state. It existed within the borders of a host nation and, at any moment, could be invaded. Then came college, its co-ed halls and bathrooms thwarting any modicum of privacy. But your individual freedoms expanded—walls and the privacy afforded by them no longer had the same bearing on behavior. You were free to do as you pleased—and you did, altogether too often. Then you graduated, moved back into your parents' home and discovered that every square inch of those two stories oppressed you. It wasn't the relics in your bedroom—the basketball trophies on the shelf or the Metallica posters you'd hung in the eighth grade that still covered the walls—so much as it was the unspoken questions, fastened like millstones to every conversational pause. Your parents didn't lack tact; they knew what not to ask. But their consideration made those silences all the more degrading. You knew what they wanted to know. What was worse, you knew that they were too goddamned polite to ask because they sensed, correctly, that you didn't know the answers. Most nights, after dinner, you fled to friends' homes, preferring the carpeted floors, dog-hair-upholstered couches and one particularly spacious walk-in closet to the comforts of your own bed—anything to avoid the tacit disapproval provoked by your habitual oversleeping.

Eventually you found a shitty job and a shitty apartment to call your own. At the time, your understanding of the social contract led you to believe that you could expect the size of your apartment to grow in proportion with your waistline as you aged. But that was three years ago. And while you'd demonstrated upward mobility—rising from a file clerk to an academic tutor—you were still without a barrier between your bed and a refrigerator, so that its implacable drone permeated your every thought, mood, dream, fantasy. Now, here you were, indulging in a rare moment of solitude.

What you figured you had in common with Bill and Amare was that you were wary of participating in a society that gave so readily to some yet withheld from others. In fact, "withhold" wasn't strong enough a word. It had to scapegoat and stigmatize those others, label them "moochers" and "drains" that would bleed us all dry if they had their way. You realized that the more you took from an inequitable system, the more you'd end up defending it. And this proposition scared you. It was the paradox of privilege—take what you need to survive until what you need to survive takes you.

What if, like Bill and Amare, you considered the things people sacrificed in order to align their identities with their desires—integrity, empathy, humility, humanity, time—too precious? What if you were to say: No. No, I will not participate in that. No, I do not want what you want. No, even at the risk of going childless and penniless through this cruel world and dying alone, no. No, even at the risk of being judged a failure by my peers, no. Because we all die alone. And while you weren't exactly at peace with that, at least you didn't deny it.

You extinguished your cigarette and thought: I deny it. I deny the hell out of it. You were selfish, entitled, sanctimonious, naïve. And recognizing these facts didn't make them any less true. Maybe what you needed, what all of you needed, was an ultimatum: accomplish goal A by time B or face penalty C. And the punishment had to be something worse than living in a junior one-bedroom apartment with adequate discretionary income to afford cable television. It had to be worse than occasionally needing to take a few drinks in order to get some sleep. It had to be worse than the sneaking suspicion that you were wasting valuable time.

Your cell phone vibrated in your pocket. June again. You let it go to voicemail. Survival was possible through avoidance. At that moment, the mere thought of slipping once again on her slope was all the motivation you needed to take a step forward.

You called Julia.

The conversation was halting and awkward, the two of you struggling to rediscover whatever common ground you'd found in the bar, but it ended with the arrangement of what sounded like a date—albeit one with a built-in fail-safe. Julia had two friends. She wondered if you did too.

"Of course!" you said. But this request was unfamiliar territory. In the brief history of your prosaic dating life, such a scenario had never arisen. You didn't know whether to take it as a vote of confidence (she really liked you and was betting that you were a well worth tapping), or a vote of ambivalence (she was uncertain about you, was a little drunk when she met you, and wanted the assistance of a second and third pair of eyes to help determine whether or not to give you a shot).

Per Julia's suggestion, you arranged a rendezvous for the next night at 4100 Bar, a Sunset Boulevard meat market that you hadn't patronized since 2001, during the post-college, pre-June days of testosterone-laced booty recon, nights when 12:30 would roll around and you, Harrison, and your buzzes would abandon whatever dive you'd been posted in so that you might have a chance to lay claim to some unattached beer-goggle beauty who was beginning to fear that she'd worn the sexy underwear for nothing.

You hung up and began a mental inventory of your friends, calculating which ones would allow you to shine and ruling out those whose personalities and/or good looks might outshine your own. When Bill and Amare returned a few minutes later from the store bearing groceries, you were so carried away by the gesture of generosity that you suggested they clip their fingernails, iron their nicest shirts, and come meet some pretty girls.

"You're serious?" said Bill.

Amare laughed. "One of your students drop a textbook on your head?"

"I thought you'd be stoked."

"Is that pizza communal?" said Bill.

"Eat!" you said.

They grabbed slices, disregarded the paper towels you'd left out, and, with the grace and fluidity of gymnasts dismounting a pair of balance beams, kicked off their shoes, flipped on the television and planted their asses on the couch.

"I mean, don't get me wrong, Josh," said Bill through a mouthful of cheese and dough. "I'm grateful for the vote of confidence. But I'd sooner subject myself to a rectal examination than the disappointed face of some aspiring actress who's hoping to get paired up with a handsome studio executive and winds up sitting across from me."

"You feel this way too?" you said to Amare.

"I get enough disappointment when I call home."

You felt like you were trying to convince them to join you at a Howard Dean rally—it was probably the right thing to do, but being right didn't assuage the embarrassment caused by such a public acknowledgment of desperation. "I think that you shouldn't wait for your life to look a certain way before you start looking for some companionship," you said. "Who knows what's waiting for us out there? You might meet the person that inspires you to change your life; you might meet the person that helps you make peace with the life you have."

The boys chewed pensively, their eyes lost in the images of ice-cold beer and scantily clad women that paraded across the muted television screen.

"Talk to girls," said Amare.

"That's all you'll have to do!" you said. "We're getting back on the horse! We don't need to get laid, we just need to put ourselves in situations where the possibility, however remote, exists!"

Bill retrieved a second slice of pizza. "Do you mind if I grab one of these beers?"

"Drink!" you said.

"Now there's a cause I can get behind."

*

THE NEXT DAY WAS a slow one at The Homework Club. The study room was sparsely populated. With no Adrienne present you felt less necessary, a brain in possession of fleetingly coveted information. Tim received his private students in his office while Eric, on location with Haley Joel Osmont, waited like a kept woman in his trailer to lavish an LA Unified–approved tenth grade curriculum upon his movie-star client. You helped two boys—the son of the man who had taken issue with Sophie's salacious photo, a seventh-grader prone to staring blankly from behind long black bangs and making strange clicking sounds with his tongue, and another middle-schooler who smelled of burnt hair and had ravaged his fingernails down to jagged nubs—with their pre-algebra homework. In between problems you watched the clock, pressed your fist into the ever-tightening knot in your gut, and anxiously awaited Sophie's arrival. In the past, you would have backed off the stance you'd taken yesterday, made some crack about a lack of sleep and caffeine, assured her that you didn't care what she brought into the study room as long as she didn't distract the other kids from their work. Today you intended to do the opposite. How could you face a triple-date on the same day that you'd backed down from a seventeen-year-old girl, regardless of the way her hair smelled or the color of her eyes?

At 6:30 the Chevy Chevette that Amare had bought the week before for $900 pulled up to the curb outside the front door. White with glued-on wood panels, the thing required a quart of motor oil every time he stopped for gas. You gave it three months, provided Amare kept it within the city limits and didn't drive on the freeway. Which you guessed suited him just fine. Amare's Los Angeles sojourn reeked of impermanence.

You left the bewildered middle-school boys to their own devices and went outside. The air was thick, the day's heat having trapped the smog in the Valley the way an argument with June used to trap a scream in your throat. Bill opened the passenger door, stepped onto the sidewalk, and stretched. He'd showered, shaved, gotten what remained of his hair cut, and dressed in a navy blue button-down shirt of yours that was comically large on him—shoulder stitching hanging halfway to his elbows, sleeves bunched up at the wrists.

"My, my," you said. "Don't you clean up nice."

"Right," he said, smiling sheepishly. "*Celebrity Makeover* has been banging down the door all morning." He pulled the shirt away from his chest a few times to air himself out. "Christ, it's hot. I haven't even had to defend my employment status yet and already I'm sweating."

"Who gives a shit?" you said. "It's ninety-six degrees. We're men, aren't we?"

"I told him not to go fishing around in your closet," said Amare, walking around the front of the car to join you on the sidewalk. His paunch didn't allow his red checkered shirt to fall more than an inch past his belt. He'd neglected to shave but it didn't matter. His brown skin ameliorated the scragglyness of his beard, making the barren patches on his face look intentional.

Bill hung his head. "My only button-down shirt has tartar sauce on it. It looks like a cum stain."

"You look great," you said. "Both of you."

"We were down the street, getting the back of Bill's neck shaved," said Amare. "Thought we should swing by to see if you had any more information for us."

"I haven't heard from Julia," you said. "You guys should head home for a couple hours and relax."

"There's beer there," said Amare.

"Good," you said. "Have a couple cold ones."

Amare chewed his lip. "You sure you don't need any help in there? You have any students that would benefit from a crash course in the illegitimacy of the US occupation of Iraq?"

You chuckled.

"Seriously."

"You terrify children," said Bill.

"We've got to get to them while they're young," said Amare. "Before they become utterly dependent on cheap gas, online shopping, and PlayStation."

"Eric, my boss…he supports the war," you said.

"Are you fucking kidding me?"

You stuffed your hands in your pockets. "It really caught me off guard. I mean, he can be a dick sometimes, but he's got a brain."

"You see? How are we supposed to have any kind of hope for the future of this country when our educators, you know, learned people, endorse an illegal war?"

Bill looked over your shoulder and his jaw dropped. "Ugh," he said, as though he'd been slugged in the gut. "There's hope for this country yet."

You pivoted. Sophie glided toward you. Books tucked under her arm, backpack slung over her shoulder, her blond hair swished back and forth, shimmering like light caught by the ocean.

"I would marry her right now," Bill said softly, safely beneath the drone of traffic. "No questions asked. She could be a raging cunt who forbade whiskey drinking and the viewing of Red Sox games. I wouldn't care."

Sophie raised her blue eyes from the sidewalk and met yours. She frowned. Then, as if struck by an epiphany, she stopped, scrutinized Bill and Amare, and spread her lips into the kind of beatific smile that graces toothpaste ads.

"Are these your friends, Josh?"

"How was school, kiddo?"

She made a noise, a quick, forced, contemptuous exhalation. "Can you believe the rudeness?" she said to Bill. "He doesn't even introduce me."

You sighed. "Sophie."

"I'm Bill." Bill took a step forward, wiped his palm on your blue button-down shirt and extended his hand. "It's nice to meet you, Sophie."

Her plump lips closed over her teeth and she grinned coquettishly. "Very nice to meet you too, Bill," she said, shaking his hand. "It's nice to see that at least Josh's friends have manners." She turned to Amare.

He nodded. "Hey," he mumbled with a barely perceptible lift of his chin.

Sophie smiled weakly and returned her gaze to Bill. "How about this heat, huh?"

"I know," said Bill. "Two minutes outside and I'm like a steamed lobster."

She rolled her head back on her shoulders and laughed.

"Seriously," said Bill. "Drop me in a bisque and charge market price."

She covered her mouth with her hand. "You're funny," she gasped.

Bill looked at his feet.

"Sophie," you said. "Why don't you go inside? I'll just be a minute."

"Josh hates me," she said to Bill.

"Josh doesn't hate anyone," said Bill.

"It's true," she said.

"She's right," you said.

Her jaw dropped. Amare chuckled. Having disarmed her of her smile, you continued. "Sophie and I disagreed about something, so now I hate her. Where just yesterday, I believed her to be a kind, beautiful, talented person, now, because of a single disagreement, our friendship is over."

She regained her composure, that smile spreading again across her face, and her spine straightening until she stood before you like a flagpole. "So you think I'm beautiful?"

Your mouth went dry. You rubbed your neck where your carotid artery had begun pumping blood at such a furious clip that you feared it might be visible to the naked eye. You laughed as though she had said something amusing, said, "Ain't she a character, fellas?" and cleared your throat in a vain attempt to muster saliva. The looks leveled at you by Bill and Amare reminded you of the face of a childhood friend the day that the two of you were caught stealing cigarettes from a drug store. "Go inside, Soph. We'll tackle that English essay first thing."

Chin raised, beatific smile restored, she said, "Okay, Josh. You're the boss. Nice to meet you, Josh's friends."

They mumbled goodbyes and The Homework Club door closed behind her like a coffin lid.

"Christ," said Amare.

"I don't know how you do it," said Bill. "I'd be gunned down by her father inside a week."

"I can't believe I said that."

"You're fine," said Amare. "You can defuse this."

"I called her beautiful."

"Well she is!" said Amare. "And she knows it! All you did was confirm what she already knew. Acknowledging a fact and acting on it are two very separate things."

You were unconvinced. Acknowledging something with words felt tantamount to action. You sent the boys packing, assured them that you would call as soon as you had word of the impending date and returned to work.

You avoided Sophie most of the evening, letting her gossip with the gaggle of girls that showed up for the second study-room session and mess around with her cell phone. You worried about Adrienne. It wasn't like her to be absent for consecutive days without calling. While she'd never really gotten into trouble, she did have some of the characteristics of a powder keg. You'd shrugged off your fears in the past, figuring that she would wait until college to let loose. But what if some influence, say a tutor who treated her too much like an equal, who identified with her and spoke a little too openly with her, burdening her with ideas that he himself was too afraid to incorporate into his life, urged her one too may times to unfetter herself of the constraints of the uberachiever? Is that what you were supposed to teach? That her parents didn't know what was best for her? You were a tutor, not a guidance counselor.

Shortly before locking up, you received the text from Julia. You texted Amare directions to the bar where the six of you were to meet, then adjourned to the bathroom to splash some water on your face, check your teeth for food particles, and tell your skeptical reflection that you knew who the fuck you were.

*

4100 BAR WAS AS you remembered it: dark, crowded, velvety, loud. In the gloom and from a distance, you could easily have mistaken Julia for her short brunette friend if Julia hadn't been Chinese. On closer inspection, the brunette had the slight potbelly and waxen complexion of an aspiring lush. Friend number two was a six-foot blond Amazon who didn't quite have Sophie's stunning eyes, but was otherwise a fair approximation of what Sophie might grow into in five years time.

You and Julia hugged. Lavender filled your nostrils as your hands discovered the sinewy muscles of her back and arms. Thundering hip-hop made formal introductions impossible, so you crossed your fingers and smiled politely as Bill and Amare shook hands with Julia's friends.

"You look nice," you said.

She leaned in close and turned her ear towards you.

"What?"

"You! Look! Nice!"

She smiled. You gestured towards a crescent booth in the corner that appeared large enough to accommodate six. Julia led the way and you followed, Bill walking beside the aspiring lush, and Amare paired, by virtue of height, with the Amazon. Along the way, you stopped at the bar. You and the Amazon opened separate tabs.

Why Julia had chosen this place was beyond you. It was too dark and too loud for her friends to form an impression of you. You hoped that she simply had no better ideas. After all, it wasn't as if you were looking for an LA bar scene aficionado. The chief qualities you sought were curiosity and tolerance, someone who might be initially charmed by your savvy, experience, and history of moderately self-destructive behavior, but someone who would ultimately inspire transformation, cure you of your penchant for dive bars. You knew that you'd miss it terribly— the singular excitement of embarking on a night out as a single person, drinking and driving through a make-believe realm of endless possibility. But you wanted love. And in none of your fantasies was the recipient of your love a party animal. She wasn't supposed to know the bartenders by name or get copped rounds on the house. You wanted a novice, someone comfortable amongst the corrupted, but willful and ambitious enough to resist their traps.

Bill and the lush scooted into the booth. Julia sat next to her friend and you took the edge seat beside her. Amare and the Amazon sat across from you. A popular indie rock song, prominently featured on the insufferable loop at your gym, blasted from the speakers. The lush raised her arms above her head, danced in her seat and sang along. Bill tried to smile, but the look on his face was one of acute discomfort, like a teenager being forced to pose for the family photograph. He mumbled something under his breath.

"What was that?" she said. She turned to you as if you were Bill's translator. "I can't hear him. What did he say?"

You pointed to your ears, feigned deafness.

"It's not important," yelled Bill. "Never mind."

"Are you a mumbler?" she yelled.

"No," he mumbled.

Her lip curled up into a snarl. She looked him up and down. "You are!" she yelled. "You're a total mumbler."

"I'm a grumbler!" yelled Bill. "It's different."

"How so?"

"Mumblers lack confidence. I lack volume and positivity."

"Are you joking?" She turned to you again. "Is he joking, or what?"

Your mouth opened but you had no words.

"Of course I'm joking," yelled Bill. You smiled, dabbed at the beads of sweat that had gathered on your forehead with a cocktail napkin. "I lack confidence too."

Amare was too engaged with the Amazon to note the tension. Julia's puzzled gaze lingered indiscreetly, first on Bill and then Amare, as she sipped her drink. She looked at you, took a breath and then went back to the boys. You thought that maybe her confusion, if that's what it was, wasn't totally unwarranted. Maybe you weren't exactly the man that your grooming and manners and vocabulary conveyed. Maybe the guys you'd brought along to pair up with her two friends, with their sarcasm and their frumpiness and their joblessness and their indigence, were a little closer on the outside to what she was beginning to suspect was on the inside of you.

She broke the lull with a question. "I was wondering," she said, "what made you want to become a teacher?"

It was precisely the kind of question you'd hoped she'd start with. It gave you a reference point, indicated how deep you'd gone the other night at The Burrow, how much personal history had been divulged.

"I'm really not a teacher," you said.

"Tutoring is teaching," she said.

"I guess."

"Come on," she said, giving your side a little jab with her elbow. "Stop being modest."

You smiled. "It happened by accident. I never intended to be a tutor…teacher…whatever."

She snorted. "You think that makes you any different from the rest of us?"

"No. I…what?"

"How many of us out there are what we expected to be?"

"Right. I realize that most people…"

"What did you *intend* to be?" she said.

You winced. You drained what was left of your beer. "I think I'd rather not say."

She rolled her eyes.

"An actor," you said. "I thought I'd be an actor."

"Well there's nothing unusual there."

"I realize that."

"Oh. That's the problem, right? You want to be different."

"Don't you?"

"I want to be happy," she said.

"Yeah. I want that. I mean, happiness is more important than originality for sure."

She pinched the slender cocktail straws between her thumb and forefinger and took another sip of vodka cranberry. "I'll bet your parents are proud."

"I guess," you said.

"Huh?" She leaned in and cupped a hand around her ear. "What'd you say?"

"I said, 'I guess they're proud'. My parents. But proud is kind of their baseline."

She shrugged. The jukebox had begun blasting The Commodores' "Brick House" and you weren't certain she'd heard you over the funk.

You swigged the last of your beer, sucked on your empty beer bottle, placed it back on the table and folded the cardboard coaster in halves, fourths, eighths. It broke apart in your fingers. You blushed, tucked your recalcitrant hands under your thighs. Everyone knows that peeling beer labels and massacring coasters are the physical manifestations of sexual frustration and, coupled with the acting confession, you'd already given away plenty. *Why not just go ahead and reveal all your secrets,* you thought. *Tell her about the anxiety, about the amount of medication it took to get you to a place where you could hold down a job. Tell her about your hair, the amount of money you invested in pills to keep it from falling out. Tell her about June, the ex-girlfriend you still jerked off to, or how about Sophie, the seventeen-year-old student you'd had an erotic dream about a few weeks ago. Let's hear her talk about proud parents after that little revelation.*

"What about you?" you said.

"What about me?"

"Your folks, I mean. They must be proud of…of who you are."

She shrugged. "I suppose." She sipped her drink.

Your hands returned to the mangled bits of coaster. "I mean, you give the impression of being pretty grounded. Like, I don't know…I'm sure they're happy to see what a…" you cleared your throat, "what a grounded person you are."

"I'm twenty-six years old, Josh."

"Oh?"

To your left, Amare gesticulated wildly at the Amazon, drawing away Julia's attention. The way the ridge of his right hand cut the air and landed in the center of his left palm like a gavel, suggested they'd encountered a topic of contention. You'd warned Amare that these girls went to USC; you'd pleaded with him to try, if at all possible, to avoid talking politics. "Don't blow a chance to get blown just because someone's daddy raised her on Ronald Reagan and the free market," were your approximate words. The Amazon leaned back in her seat, as though Amare was talking through a megaphone, and clutched her drink for dear life.

Julia stared at her vodka-cranberry-stained ice cubes.

"Can I get you another?" you said.

"Oh," she said. "I don't think I should. I don't ordinarily drink this fast."

You glanced at Bill. He didn't appear to be doing much better. The lush was peering at him like she'd just walked into a dark room after being out in the noonday sun and was having a difficult time identifying him as human or coat rack. His nose pointed straight down at the table and she frowned at his bald dome like a shit-smeared shoe sole.

Julia sighed, looked at her watch.

"Anyway," you said. "Tutoring. I don't know what you've imagined, but it's not exactly noble work. My students are mostly privileged private school kids who're too lazy do their homework."

She looked past you, at something on the wall or a better-looking guy walking by. "Every kid deserves an education, right? Just because they've got money doesn't mean that they shouldn't have good teachers."

"Yeah, well, it's a rare day that I leave work feeling like I've made any kind of difference."

She smiled with the left side of her mouth. "You're an idealist," she said.

"Yeah, I don't know. Maybe. They say that's a symptom of youth. They say I'll be outgrowing that soon."

"What do you want me to say? Do you want me to agree that you're relatively unimpressive? Is that why you brought these two?"

You stiffened, crossed your arms over your chest. The Commodores were still blasting away and you were certain that Bill and Amare couldn't have heard anything, but you leaned in anyway.

"These are my guys," you said. "They're magnificent people." She took the straws out of her drink and took a large swallow.

"I'm serious," you said.

"I'm not saying they're not great guys."

"So what's the problem?"

"Hey Julia!" yelled the lush. "You hungry?"

"Kinda," said Julia.

"You want to try another venue?" you said. You raised your voice and addressed the table. "You guys want to go get something to eat?"

The women exchanged glances. Bill and Amare sipped the dregs of their drinks and fiddled with cocktail straws.

"Where should we go?" said Julia.

"What do you feel like eating?"

"I want a cheeseburger!" yelled the Amazon.

"Ugh," piped Bill. "I can't eat another cheeseburger."

"Are you serious?" yelled Amare.

"Can't do it."

"You've ingested like three quarters of a cow in the last week."

"I've reached my threshold."

"So we'll go to a fucking diner," yelled Amare. "You can go to a fucking diner, right? You can eat a fucking salad."

"We'll go to Mel's," you yelled. "They've got whatever you want...burgers, fries, salads. I think they even sell beer."

Julia put her hand on your thigh. Either she liked your decisiveness or the booze had created a craving for onion rings.

You settled up with the bartender. The girls insisted on paying for their own drinks and you didn't argue. As they waited for the bartender to make change, they engaged in an animated discussion with plenty of head shaking. Bill and Amare had their work cut out for them.

*

YOU SLOGGED THROUGH HOLLYWOOD Boulevard traffic toward the restaurant—four cars transporting six passengers—determined not to let the girls' insistence on driving themselves discourage you. That bar had been all wrong. Bill and Amare had no chance in a setting like that with girls like these. Irony and sarcasm were their stock-in-trade, and the music in that place had been too damn loud for them to utilize these weapons effectively.

You cut the AC and rolled down your window. Warm air lapped your face. The car next to you boomed an apocalyptic bass track through a sub-woofer that seemed eminently capable of penetrating the earth's crust and initiating the big one that would finally crumble California into the Pacific. You cranked up the volume on your own stereo, drowning the noise with Ben Webster's lascivious baritone.

Bill and Amare pulled up behind you at a red light. You watched them in your rearview mirror. Bill's forehead pressed against the passenger window like an overheated child trying to cool himself on the glass. Amare's hands danced above the steering wheel as though he were trying to shoo away a bee. He pointed to his head, smacked the side of it with the base of his palm. Bill's lips moved but his head didn't. You imagined his response—a weary and futile explanation that vanished as softly as it was spoken.

Your phone vibrated. You fished it from your pocket and discovered two missed calls, two new voicemails, both from June. Bill and Amare pulled up alongside you. Amare leaned his head out the window. "Dude. We're thinking of bailing on the diner."

"What?"

"Bill's girl hates him."

Bill jerked his head from the window, sat upright. "Hey, don't put this all on me," he said. "You're the one who said your date thought that a filibuster was some kind of abdominal exercise."

"He told his girl that the band on her tee shirt sucks."

"What?"

"Bill told the girl that the band on her tee shirt sucks."

The light turned green. "Why did you do that, Bill?"

The engine of the mammoth pick-up truck behind you growled. "Because it's the truth!" yelled Bill.

Its driver leaned on the horn. Amare didn't so much as glance, just increased his volume. "We're thinking of picking up a bottle!"

More car horns joined in a symphony of outrage.

"No fucking way!" you yelled. "Please. I can't show up there alone!"

Angry voices punctuated the horn symphony with staccato bursts of profanity.

"Trust me," yelled Amare. "They'll be relieved."

"Fuck that!" you yelled. "Don't fucking do this to me!"

You hit the gas and swerved into the lane ahead of them. They followed obediently, resuming the crawl. A thump came from the rear of your car. At the next light, as you came to a halt, there was another thump and you realized it was your basketball, careening around your trunk. You hadn't played in your regular Wednesday night pick-up game since the Homework Club had extended your hours. In fact, since Bill and Amare had started staying at your place, you'd avoided your dad's 8:00 a.m. wake-up calls and skipped the Saturday morning game too. Still balling twice a week in his late fifties, your dad was becoming a rarity. There was no telling how many opportunities you had left to run together. Dad didn't play the most physical game, but one wrong step and he'd be shopping for golf clubs.

You picked up your phone and called voicemail. The first message was nothing, a hang up. The second began with a pause, followed by an, "Oh, hi." Then another pause. As if you were the one that had called her and caught her at an inopportune time. "Well," she said. "It finally happened. Reno hit me. I can't go home because my stepdad is staying with my mom again so my sister is driving me to a hostel in Hollywood. I have enough money for two nights. After that I guess I'll start whoring myself out on Santa Monica Boulevard. I love you. Call me."

You stuffed the phone into the cup holder filled with receipts and the cardboard sleeves from take-out coffee cups. The stream of cars crossing in your path thinned out. You stared into the empty intersection, your mind thick with car exhaust and the flagging will to make sound decisions.

June was an ineluctable force. She was the rain that seeped through the cracks in your ceiling. She was the small damp circle that rapidly devolved into a dozen steady trickles and a home littered with brimming pots and pans. This message was the lightning flash before the thunderclap, the first storm after a protracted draught. You knew from experience that it would soon expose those holes that you'd been too busy, too distracted to repair during the dry time.

You should have deleted the voicemail without listening, or at least waited until tomorrow, with the possibility of new romance to steel you against temptation. Instead you'd once again demonstrated that, like alcohol and caution or Bill's mouth and his libido, June and logic existed in direct opposition to one another. And there were some things you could not unhear. June was nearly broke and homeless. The subtext—that it was only a matter of time before she showed up on your doorstep—was easy enough to glean. Your life was a Greek tragedy; your most laudable quality, your compassion, would be the instrument of your demise. Two paths lay before you. The first was full retreat—a mad dash through the Hollywood Hills to the safety of a Valley, a couch, a bottle, and unabashed shit-talking. You'd lost sight of Julia's Audi anyway. Perhaps this was merely the path of fate's acceptance. Down the second was Mel's Diner and whatever promise was conveyed in that small but significant gesture—Julia's fingertips tracing circles on your thigh. It was not lost on you that sex might be a powerful inoculation against June's lure.

You stayed the course.

*

YOU WERE SOMEWHAT EMBARRASSED for having suggested Mel's Diner, a crowded and cacophonous eatery plagued by tourists and high school students. You prided yourself on your knowledge of off-the-beaten-path restaurants and dive bars, and yet you'd chosen this tacky, run-of-the-mill chain smack in the heart of Hollywood. What was worse, its patrons' affinity for

Tommy Hilfiger accentuated Bill and Amare's otherness, their lack of conventional effort.

You spotted an empty table near the back, navigated the churning cauldron of douche bags—whose busy hands shoveled curly fries into their meticulously manicured faces or plunged beneath tabletops to grope the exposed thighs of their dates—and seated yourselves. The lush and the Amazon continued a debate that must have started in the car about Los Angeles Lakers star Kobe Bryant and whether or not they would have stood by him after he allegedly raped a hotel employee in Denver.

"Kobe Bryant," muttered Bill, as if the words themselves were acid on his tongue.

"Excuse me?" said the lush. "Did you say something?"

"A portrait of a gentleman if I ever saw one."

Amare chuckled. "That team is chock full of assholes, from the coach on down."

"What are you talking about?" said the Amazon. "Phil Jackson is like the best coach in the history of the NBA."

You and Amare scoffed. Julia looked at you sideways.

"Hasn't he won the most championships?" she said. "Doesn't that make him the best?"

You shrugged. "That's a little like saying the richest man in the room is also the smartest."

The Amazon snorted. "Well if that rich man owned a basketball team, he'd be an idiot not to hire Phil fregging Jackson."

The lush laughed. "Nice," she said, holding up her hand. The Amazon gave her a vigorous high-five.

A harried waitress, looking either ten years too old or thirty years too young to be working the late shift at a chain diner, surfaced beside your table, the dull tip of her pencil poised just above her order pad. The girls ordered fries and Diet Cokes.

You went with a beer. Amare ogled the beer and wine list and then asked for water.

Bill scratched his whiskered cheeks. "Does the grilled cheese come with a salad?"

"Fries, fruit, or side salad," said the waitress.

"Can I get the goat cheese and walnut salad with the grilled cheese, or is that extra?"

The waitress raised her eyes from her order pad to Bill. "That's not a side salad."

Bill held the menu with one hand and rubbed his bald dome with the other. "How much would you charge me if I got the grilled cheese with the walnut salad?"

She peered at him over the rim of her reading glasses. "I wouldn't charge you anything, but the restaurant would charge you the full price of the grilled cheese plus the full price of the salad."

Bill sighed. "Forget it." He dropped the menu and scanned the table. He rifled through the artificial sweeteners. "Don't you guys have any crackers or anything? I'd be fine with some crackers and an ice water."

The waitress frowned. "I"ll be right back with your drinks," she said and headed off toward the kitchen.

"For fuck's sake," said Amare.

"What?" said Bill. "My blood sugar is low. You want me to go into diabetic shock over here?"

Amare laughed.

"Jesus," said the lush. "Do you guys even like each other?"

Julia and the Amazon snickered. "Seriously," she said. "All they do is bicker. They're worse than my parents."

"Look, sweetheart," said Amare. "This is a good man. I love this man. I've just seen an awful lot of him lately."

Bill stared sheepishly at the table, his cheeks tinged red.

"Did you guys move here together?" said Julia.

"Amare came first," said Bill. "People were bailing out of Olympia like a sinking ship and I couldn't think of anything better to do. All I knew was that any place was better than there."

The lush's lips curled in disgust. "That's a pretty stupid reason for moving."

"Yeah, well, I didn't mean to give anyone the impression that I was anything other than stupid. Josh over there is the teacher. I was just hoping to look halfway intelligent by proxy."

The waitress brought your beer. Amare licked his lips.

"I think we're gonna need two more of these," you said.

Amare patted your shoulder. "Bless you."

"Do you have whiskey?" said Bill.

"Only beer and wine," said the waitress.

Bill scanned the beer and wine list as though it might belie the waitress' claim. "I'd kiss Kobe Bryant's feet for a glass of whiskey."

The lush sneered. "You're full of shit."

The waitress brightened and looked back and forth from the lush to Bill, her lips slightly parted.

Bill looked up from the wine list; his eyebrows climbed his forehead. "Excuse me?"

The lush sat straight as a rod. "You act like you don't give a shit but you do. You just want to look like you're not trying so you can look down your nose at anybody who is."

Bill smiled. "Everyone's entitled to their opinion. If you want to think that…"

"I do!" she said, smacking the table. "That's exactly what I think."

Now the waitress looked at you. You shrugged. A smile spread across her face like a sunrise across a meadow. "I'll be right back with your drinks."

Bill sighed. He tossed the wine list toward the center of the table. "Look," he said. "I'm sorry I insulted your tee shirt."

"I don't care about the fucking tee shirt!" said the lush. "I want to know why I'm wasting an evening with a guy who doesn't seem to have anything positive to say about *anything*. I mean, don't you have *dreams*? Isn't there anything at all that you want to *do* with your life?"

Bill shrugged. "I don't know." An impish grin tugged at the corners of his mouth. "Work at a grocery store?"

You and Amare erupted into laughter. The lush's wan cheeks burned scarlet. Julia turned her head, as if averting her gaze from a gruesome car accident. You wiped tears from your eyes.

*

AFTER THE MEAL YOU lingered outside Mel's with Julia, shuffling your feet. Highland Avenue bustled with late night traffic. Car horns honked, people whistled, the heads of drunken teenagers popped out of overstuffed cars to harass girls in neighboring cars. Julia's friends motored off down the sidewalk, high-heels clicking defiantly against concrete; Amare and Bill vanished in search of liquor. You surprised Julia by going in for a hug. You put you arms around her and she stood there stiffly for a beat before slowly, reluctantly, raising her arms halfway up your back. When you let go, she was wearing the kind of plastered-on smile that people wear when they've been cornered by a TV reporter and a question they really don't want to answer.

"This was fun," you said.

She looked at you like you'd just belched beer breath in her face.

"Seriously," you said.

She patted your arm. "Drive safe, Josh."

You lit a cigarette and strolled to your car, exhaling languid clouds that engulfed your head in the lazy heat. You slumped into the driver's seat, rolled down the window and flicked the butt onto the asphalt. You dialed June. She answered on the first ring.

"Hey, love."

*

LOOKING BACK, YOU COULDN'T remember making too many decisions when it came to June. Your rational brain had been marginalized the moment you slept with her and recognized you had something to which you would go to great lengths to preserve. This recognition led to a series of ultimatums. *Move in with me or we're finished*, was one of many in a catalog that included: *if you leave now to go play basketball, I'll burn your books; if you touch me, I'll scream; if you call my brother, I'll hurt you; if you call my mother, I'll hurt myself.*

Move out now or we will evict you, was the ultimatum that finally saved you, or at least saved your duodenum from those precocious peptic ulcers that, at the tender age of twenty-three, were beginning to wreak havoc on your digestive system. The threat to evict followed a couple of months in which June's sister April had illicitly taken up residence at your apartment. A sweet, skinny nineteen-year-old photography student at Santa Monica City College, April was a seemingly innocuous addition to the apartment—she slept late, listened to reggae, and ate cereal three times a day. Eager to help her out of June's dysfunctional family home—and hopeful that April's presence might mitigate some of the tension in your own—you had offered her a room. But April was nearly broke and contributed very little financially. Unable to afford the bump in rent that would result from adding a third person to the lease, you and June tried to keep her presence a secret. Unfortunately, loud arguments at all hours of the night had not endeared the two of you to anyone attempting to sleep in close proximity. The neighbors ratted you out and the managers gave you a month to vacate the building. June was ready to fight; you were ready to flee.

This fact may have crystallized the difference between you—not necessarily that June was a fighter and you were a capitulator, but that when it came to your life, you took the long-view, perhaps thinking of life after June and preferring to imagine it without PTSD and a severely impaired credit rating. Whatever her faults, June was invested in life's every moment with every fiber of her myopic heart, and it was this quality, more so than her skills in the sack or her physical beauty, that so hopelessly attracted you. You marveled at her emotions, at how raw and volatile they were. You couldn't believe how she fought you; you couldn't believe how she fought for you.

Answers tend to lie in the past, and June's past was no riddle. Her father died under suspicious circumstances when she was a toddler. For months June carried around his black patent leather shoes that she could see her reflection in, holding them up for her mother and brother and asking when Daddy was coming home. Things went from bad to worse when June was five years old and the man who had been repeatedly questioned in connection with her dad's untimely death moved in with her mother. Young June sought vengeance. She hid his car keys, flushed his cigarettes down the toilet, and feigned nightmares so her mother would be forced to sleep in her bed.

You'd met the stepfather just once, shortly after you and June moved in together. It was the lone occasion on which you visited June's mother's house. You spent an hour in the kitchen with June's mom while the stepdad watched the Lakers in the living room. He kept his distance and you didn't have the chance to form much of an impression, but you fundamentally distrusted any man who requested that his wife bring him a beer while she was with company; June's stepfather pulled off a hat trick, achieving this feat three times in a single hour. Meanwhile, June's mother kept at least one cigarette burning and her hand rarely left the neck of a bottle of chilled white wine. She leaned against the kitchen counter, lowered her designer frames to the bridge of her nose, and propped a hand on her waist, gold bangles sliding down her forearm to her wrist. She looked you up and down, pointed the ruby red fingernail of her index finger at your face. In a heavy Filipino accent, she said, "He's is handsomer than the last one. And tall." Then she appraised her daughter. She touched June's delicate chin, pinched her attenuated arm. "She still my most beautiful child, but too skinny. You make sure she eat?"

"She's picky, but when she has what she wants…"

"Always picky," agreed her mom, still scrutinizing her daughter. "Always so much work."

For the rest of the visit, she lavished you with booze and compliments and congratulated her daughter on having found a nice young man who was willing to put up with her moods. You swilled enough Chardonnay to mitigate the discomfort caused by her passive aggressive compliments and impair your ability to operate a motor vehicle. During the ride home, you

rolled down the passenger window, hoping to the fresh air
might encourage June to breathe deeply and shake it off, but
by the time she turned the car onto your street, she'd gnashed
her fingernails down to bloody nubs. She parked the car but
made no move to unbuckle her seatbelt. So the two of you sat
for a while in silence. There was nothing you could say that
would make it better. All you could do was resolve to make use
of the memory, summon it as a shortcut to the well of patience
and forgiveness that living with her required. You didn't know
if she'd taken you there with the hope that things might be
different, or if she had done it to shame you, to make you feel
guilty for having a supportive and loving family. In the end, you
decided that the answer was neither. June opened a window
into her life so she could close it permanently, so you would
stop asking questions, so that, bound to her by the knowledge
of the wrecked home from which she had fled, you would help
create a home she could rely on, one you would never leave.

And yet leave you did. Following the eviction threat and
a weeklong maelstrom of invectives hurled like pointed stones
and dishes shattered like fragile egos, your cohabitation
was officially euthanized. You'd lived together for a year,
neglecting friendships, emptying savings accounts, and casting
ignominious shadows over your resumes in the form of
unexplainable absences from the work force. That you each
privately blamed yourselves was of little consequence. In the
arena of break-ups, preservation of self-worth reigned supreme.
Yours was a relationship that had left each participant well
armed with examples of the other's treachery; neither of you
were willing to grant the other any measure of mercy. So, like
a pair of howling dogs trying to smother a siren's wail, you

exchanged insults ceaselessly, just as you had once uttered oaths of everlasting love.

*

AFTER THE TRIPLE-DATE WITH Bill and Amare had gone Hiroshima, you called June and received a full update. She'd fled her abusive interim boyfriend, but she had not gone to a hostel in Hollywood, and she had not turned tricks on Santa Monica Boulevard. In the three-day interval between her first call to you and your return phone call, she had taken up with another man, an older man, an older Italian man by the name of Dean who once-upon-a-peptic-ulcer had spirited her away from your apartment under the auspices of lunch, only to deposit her, four hours later, with five thousand dollars worth of designer clothing and promises of a business trip to Milan where he would make her the toast of the fashion industry. At the time June had assured you that the older, wealthier, dapperer Dean was gay, but you hadn't bought that story for a second. LA was chock full of straight men who kept weekly appointments with their aestheticians for eyebrow plucks and moisturizing tips. And five thousand dollars told a very simple story. You told her that you couldn't prevent her from going to Milan, but that if she did, you wouldn't be waiting around for her when she returned. She chewed your ass out, said you were pathetic and insecure, that you'd never supported her the way she deserved to be supported, but her performance moved you about as much as a human-interest story on disenfranchised sex offenders. If this supposed benefactor really wanted to help her modeling career, he didn't need to take her to Milan to do it. Now it seemed that old Dean had finally gotten what he wanted—a tough pill to swallow.

With your prospects of new romance having just gone up in smoke, you sat in your car and listened to June say that she was happy to hear from you, that she would love to see you as soon as possible, but that, owing to Dean's generosity, she might not need your help after all. If this was a ploy, it worked. You abandoned Bill and Amare to their booze quest and drove straight to Dean's West Hollywood home.

The adobe-style house was located on a quiet, moonlit block just south of Sunset Boulevard. Set far back from the street, a stone pathway bisected a desert garden filled with a variety of scrubs and cacti. A lone, stumpy palm tree, that didn't quite reach the roof of the house, stood like a sentry outside the red front door. You were halfway up the path, head down, hands stuffed into your pockets like it was the dead of winter and not still eighty sultry degrees outside, when a hush fell over the voices in your head and your hollow footsteps echoed in your ears like the final weary beats of a diseased heart. You stared at the red door; behind it June's laugh surfaced like a gasp from some deep oceanic trench in your brain. You froze. How long would it take to drown your feelings for her? Your attachment seemed to have no memory of the cold, dark, desolate waters under which it had been interred.

The front door opened on the older, dapperer, wealthier would-be rescuer. "You must be Josh." A glass of red wine cupped in his right hand, he extended his left hand in a flaccid greeting. "So nice to finally meet you. You have any trouble finding us?"

You dropped his hand and shuddered with orgasmic enmity, his use of the word *us* infusing you with the sanctimony of a guilty man, exonerated by some other, more egregious offender.

"No," you said. "I grew up here."

"Of course. Yes. June told me that you moved back home to be an actor. How's that going?"

Your mouth went dry. "Should I come inside?" you croaked.

"Of course!" Dean stepped aside and swept his hand through the air. "Come inside! By all means!"

The furniture was a modern collection of chrome and leather. The room's acute angles and polished surfaces conveyed the kind of taste that required an investment of time and money. June sat on an armless, moss-green leather sofa with a haughty upward tilt to it reminiscent of its owner's posture. Encased in tight blue jeans, her legs folded under her like a switchblade; she smoked a cigarette demurely, her head turned to the side so that her long dark brown hair served as a veil, hiding the black eye that had driven her into this vulture's nest.

You hovered in the middle of the room, hesitant to sit. June faced you, full lips curving slightly upward toward those high cheekbones, but her gaze fell short of meeting yours. The swelling around her eye had gone down, leaving behind a purplish-yellow semi-circle on her olive skin. It hurt you to look, to see the violence to which you'd abandoned her. She never would have ended up with that asshole if you had been the dependable man that you'd advertised yourself to be. It was true that she'd tried to provoke you, to hurt you, to reduce you to a state of perpetual jealousy and prove that you'd never taken her seriously as a partner, but she had never not loved you.

"Hey," you said. "I thought you wanted to see me."

June emitted a single sarcastic laugh. The same laugh that she used to aim like a dart at the spot in your chest where she estimated your self-doubt dwelled. But where that laugh had once possessed all the contempt needed to drive you to the brink, it now sounded hollow and helpless, as if she couldn't muster the strength to pretend anymore, as if she was too tired to communicate anything other than abject fear.

"You want me to go?" you said, pointing at the door. "I've had a long night. If you want me to go, I will."

Your host froze behind you and, in his held breath, you sensed a man on the cusp of exactly what he desired.

"No." She extinguished her cigarette. "Stay."

Dean cleared his throat. "Would you like anything to drink? There might be some beer in the fridge from my last dinner party if you'd like to have a beer."

"I'll have what you're having."

"This is a Napa Valley Pinot Noir. Two-tousand-one."

"You know what?" you said. "Never mind. Beer is fine."

Dean winked. "Outstanding."

You sat on the couch beside her. "Jesus," you said. "This thing is more comfortable than it looks."

"He paid like four thousand dollars for it."

You leaned forward, rested your forearms on your thighs and clasped your hands. "You can come home with me," you said. "My apartment is literally bursting at the seams, but we'll make room."

Her head sagged. A tear fell from her face and thwacked the soft green leather. "You don't want that," she said.

You sat up and touched her shoulder. "Of course I do."

"Then why'd it take you three days to call me back?"

You took a breath as if to speak and then closed your mouth. You'd had no good reason for waiting. You didn't try to fabricate one either. If you lied now, not only would she know that you were lying, she'd know you were willing to lie in order to absolve yourself of guilt. You might just as well wear a sign.

Dean peeked his head back into the living room. "I'm afraid there's no beer after all."

"All good, man. I don't need a drink."

"Nonsense." He disappeared back into the kitchen. "We might have some whiskey…"

June rubbed her eyes with the sleeve of her sweatshirt. "I'll come with you if that's really what you want."

You put your arms around her. She folded like an umbrella, long and thin and slight. "Of course I do," you whispered. "Of course I want you to come with me."

Dean reemerged and winced. You smiled, savoring his expression, and decided that you were going to take things one step further, punish the man, demonstrate your power.

"I'll wait in the car," you said. You looked at Dean. "Take as long as you need."

Dean cleared his throat. "What's this then?" He faced June.

"Dean," she said. "Thanks for being such a good friend."

You spied her bulging duffel bag behind the couch and retrieved it while Dean stood by like that stumpy palm tree outside his house—ornamental, useless, and rat-infested. You extended your fist for a bump. "You the man, Dean-o. Good looking out."

Dean nodded, blind to your offering. You smacked his back, hard. "Take care." Without looking back, you hefted her bag and walked out the door. Orpheus didn't have shit on you.

You sat in your car, studying your reflection in the side mirror, enjoying a victory smoke, while the distant traffic sang a mellifluous melody. The thrill of cruelty surged through your veins, as you pictured a hopeless Dean losing an argument to a man who wasn't even there. After a few minutes, June emerged. She closed the red door behind her, scanned the street, spotted your car, and crossed the stone pathway with her chin down. She slid into the passenger seat weightlessly, a mosquito landing on still water. The two of you sat in the heavy silence of an all-too-familiar world, your heart thumping in your chest. Your keys dangled from the ignition but you made no move to start the engine.

"You're sure you've got everything?"

She looked away, out the passenger window. "You think you're making a mistake. You want to be a good guy but you're scared I'm going to wreck your life." She turned toward you, her eyes huge and sparkling and scared. "I can't live with your resentment. I'd rather go back inside with that slimeball."

"I thought you liked that guy."

"He wanted me to sleep with him." She picked her nails. "Can you believe that? I just got the crap beaten out of me and he expects me to fuck him in exchange for a place to crash."

"Motherfucker," you said through clenched teeth. "I could go back in there."

She smiled, flattered by your anger. "I slept on the couch. He didn't try anything."

"There's no couch space at my place," you said. "If you come back with me, we'll be sleeping in the same bed."

"Well duh. That's part of the appeal, right?"

Your groin tingled. She leaned over and threw her arms around your shoulders. Her warm breath was on your neck.

"I'm sorry," she whispered. "I'm sorry for asking for this, for putting you in this position, for being such a bitch when you walked into Dean's. This is all just so embarrassing."

"No," you said. "It's okay. There's nothing to be embarrassed about. We've survived tougher spots. Everything's gonna be fine."

*

JUNE MOVED IN AND Amare and Bill stayed. It was clear that they felt guilty, but they truly had no other options. That first week, days started slowly. June slept late; she always had when times were toughest. And even with a hard-luck story like the one she carried around, being broke and living out of a suitcase at her already overpopulated ex-boyfriend's junior one-bedroom apartment—with a black eye courtesy of her most recent failed relationship—qualified as dire. While she slumbered into the early afternoon hours, you and the boys walked the Valley streets. You had never really explored your neighborhood on foot before, at least not without the intention of arriving at a particular nearby destination; but you didn't have to be at The Homework Club until three in the afternoon and the boys didn't have to be anywhere ever, so, rather than stay home and watch wall-to-wall 9/11 anniversary disaster porn, you took advantage of the weather and did some reconnaissance. One day you discovered a used bookstore that you'd thought had gone out of business but had just relocated. Another time you happened upon a little theater you'd never heard of that was running a production of Neil Simon's *Brighton Beach Memoirs*. You recognized a couple of the older actors' faces on the playbill—talented people who were once regulars on hit sitcoms, refugees of an industry rotten with six-pack abs and every "ism" under the sun.

Returning home, you were liable to find June, writing in her journal at the kitchen table. Bill and Amare would bring offerings—mini chocolate donuts and flavored coffee with cream and half a dozen sugars—to which June would respond with a deluge of "thank yous" and European-style cheek kissing that turned your stomach. The boys were newly adopted family.

You'd leave for work around two o'clock, hoping that Adrienne, who'd gone AWOL for a few days, would return with some scathing observation about a teacher that she loathed or a question about Burroughs or some such iconoclastic hero of subversive American youth. You'd come to depend on your talks—the way you needed to work to earn her respect, the way she nodded in approval when you made a salient argument that she had not yet considered. In her stead, you had a healthy dose of Sophie. Your fear that she might avoid the Homework Club had not come to pass. Instead she continued to flirt, to push boundaries with poorly constructed innuendo and ludicrous winks that insinuated your partnership in some kind of conspiracy.

At the end of your workdays, Bill, Amare, and June greeted you with bleary eyes, body odor, and a burgeoning degree of certainty that they and their destinies had converged, that as long as the adult world did not pursue them, they were not going to waste any energy pursuing it. Then, one unassuming Wednesday, the monotony was broken.

The day began slowly enough, with muted farts (there was a lady among you now) and muttered condolences: "You're up already too? Ugh." When the cupboards and refrigerator turned up nothing, you and the boys decided to head to Jack's Grill—the burger stand that had been satiating their voracious appetites for several weeks—for what Bill referred to as "brunch." You were introduced to the owner, Abdal, an Armenian with a thick accent, an egregious comb-over, and furry forearms. Abdal expressed his shock at having not seen this purported bachelor who lived around the corner.

"You should be my number one most best customer," he said. "This man," he said, pointing at Bill. "This man is my most best hero. He looks small but eats like giant."

Bill blushed. "I'm a stress eater."

"Stress!" yelled Abdal. "It is beautiful sunny day outside. What you have to be stress about?"

"I need a job, Abdal."

Abdal stroked his thin mustache. "Ah. This is worries me. All the time when I have no job, I am thinking, 'I am not a man,'" he said, tapping his chest with his fist.

Bill shrugged. "Yeah, well that's a sensation I'm pretty familiar with, Abdal. All the time when I have no job I am thinking, 'my teachers were right.'"

"My friend, you eat double chili cheeseburger. You feel better. More like man."

"He keeps eating double chili cheeseburgers, he will be more man," said Amare. "That's for sure."

Your burger was as good as advertised, a thick, greasy patty smothered in pickles and thousand island dressing that soaked through the cellophane and left your fingers glistening. You thanked Abdal, promised to come back, promised yourself just the opposite, and drifted over to the neighborhood park to lounge on splintered fitness equipment and pass gas in the shade of the eucalyptus trees. Acorn-fattened squirrels and sweat-suited senior citizens jogged circles around you while you digested, smoked, and discussed the state of your increasingly small world.

Ever since the disastrous triple-date, Bill had been fantasizing about life on the other side of those swinging double doors that led to the refrigerated storage rooms of grocery stores, where rubber mats carpeted wet concrete floors, cheeks were stung red by the cold, and breath was a perpetual mist in front of your face. He imagined himself wearing black rubber gloves, hefting crates, sorting vegetables, packing steaks, and spending breaks squatting on loading docks with a mix of immigrants, students, and young fathers in need of jobs with family health plans, all garbed in the soiled aprons and integrity of men and women who leave work with sore muscles.

"There's a Whole Foods in Valley Village," you said. "A girl I knew in high school works there. I guess she might be able to help you out."

"Dude, why didn't you say something before?" said Bill. "That would be fucking righteous."

Amare chuckled.

"The fuck you laughing at?" said Bill.

"I'm sorry," said Amare. "It's just your enthusiasm. I'm not accustomed to it. It amuses me."

"Pardon me for getting excited by the idea of not mooching off Josh anymore."

"Josh doesn't care," said Amare.

"Are you insane? Of course Josh cares!"

You were lost in thought, imagining a reunion with the Whole Foods girl and already regretting your offer to make the introduction.

"I was somewhere else," you said. "Who's nuts?"

"I was just fucking with you," said Amare. "I know we've worn out our welcome."

"What are you talking about?"

"We should have been out of your hair days ago."

"Weeks," said Bill.

"Screw that!" you said. "I need you guys. You think I want to be left alone with June?"

"I'd want to be alone with her," said Bill.

Amare shook his head. "You don't know what the hell you're talking about."

"All I'm saying," said Bill, "is, no offense Josh, I possess nothing, including my dignity, that I would not readily sacrifice to sleep with someone as smoking hot as your ex-ish girlfriend."

"Dignity is just the entry fee," you said, slinging an acorn at an audacious squirrel that had wandered too close.

While Amare and Bill continued to argue about the lengths to which they'd go to sleep with beautiful women, you drifted back to the Whole Foods girl, someone you now remembered you'd actually slept with one drunken night during college when she'd traveled up the coast to visit some mutual friends. You'd woken up the next morning on your friend's couch and, caught up in a moment of incredible gratitude, you were about to lie and tell her you'd always had a thing for her, when she kissed you, thanked you for the orgasm, put on her clothes, and walked out the door. You'd had so much respect for her in that moment. And it's not that it didn't sting a little bit, being discarded so easily, but now that you thought about it, it was a perfect memory of both a person and an experience. The sort of memory that gives life a narrative. You'd been so disarmed when, years later, she resurfaced as the amiable cashier who rang up your Honey Bunches of Oats cereal, free-trade bananas, and gastrointestinal supplements that you'd stopped shopping at that Whole Foods altogether. Your embarrassment had nothing to do with her attitude; she hadn't communicated anything remotely resembling shame. Your embarrassment stemmed from the feeling that you had no right to intrude on her life that way, to imagine that you knew something about what kind of person she was just because you knew where she worked.

Los Angeles natives all experienced their own personal diaspora, as the people they grew up with spread out across the hills, valleys, and coastal regions or migrated to the East Coast. Other than the occasional case of a former classmate popping up in a Miller Lite commercial or an episode of *CSI*, most of them disappeared entirely, existing only in memory and between the dusty covers of those yearbooks that were occasionally exhumed from bookshelves during indulgent bouts of nostalgia brought on by excessive drinking. Running into this girl at her place of work had been like having dinner with a friend whose girlfriend suddenly gets too drunk and starts revealing privileged information—like the guy's need for nipple tweaking during sex in order to cum, or his having a soft spot for the music of *NSYNC. It upset the portrait of a character that, in her proximity to you, helped shape your self image. If identity was nothing more than a story you told yourself, how were you supposed to maintain your grip on that story when the players from your past, the static ones carved into the stone of anecdotes, evolved?

"You want to head over to Whole Foods tomorrow morning?" Bill said hopefully.

"Sure," you said. "Tomorrow sounds good. I wish I had her email."

"Hey guys," said Amare. "Look."

You and Bill turned your heads towards the street. June stood near the curb, waiting for a break in the traffic. Her hair was pulled back in some kind of elaborate braid and the sun smoldered in her skin, summoning a bronze hue rendered fallow by perennially closed blinds and snoozed alarm clocks. June's face—how mesmerized by it you'd once been. You used to cup it in your hands, kiss it from its smooth forehead to its delicate chin, watch in amazement while she slept, smiled, ate, listened, laughed; you couldn't believe that such a face existed, that you had somehow earned the privilege to lose yourself in its architecture, to stare without fear of repercussion. When she had worn a look of longing or love, you had been reduced to a terrifyingly primal emotional state; you teetered on a precipice of laughter and tears with absolutely no control over which way you might fall. As she jogged across the street that day, you felt a familiar sense of pride: *that girl is looking for me.* You stood up to wave, so that you might be the envy of anyone watching, but then caught yourself. You sat back down, stared instead at the blades of yellow-brown grass between your legs.

"June!" yelled Bill. "Hey!"

You looked up in time to catch her flash an enchantmenting smile at Bill. She rarely smiled that way for you anymore. That smile was reserved for new men. No matter that it would have taken far less to charm Bill. June was egalitarian where it came to her charms—equal flirtation for all potential admirers.

"Hey boys," she said, leaning over to hug the shoulders of first Bill and then Amare. "Thanks for the note."

Amare furrowed his brow.

"No problem," said Bill. "Thought you might need a little motivation to leave behind the air conditioning."

"I know, right?" She stood next to where you sat, her arms crossed beneath her breasts.

"Y'all don't know hot until you've spent a summer in the South," said Amare. "This shit is nothing. Sit in the shade here and you're fine. But you can't escape humidity."

"You gonna sit down, sweetheart?" you said, knowing that June's fear of insects made it difficult for her to sit in the grass. She ignored you.

"Hey, June," said Bill. "You want to apply for jobs at Whole Foods with me? Josh knows some chick who works there. He's gonna introduce me."

"He does?" She glanced at you for the first time since she'd arrived.

"He does indeed," you said.

"You should do it," said Bill. "I mean...I enjoy sleeping-in and watching television all day as much as the next guy, but a job, as long as it's a job that you don't take home with you, I think it could be a good thing."

June chewed her lip, inclined her head slightly to the side. "You got a cigarette?"

"I'm all for solidarity as an instrument of change," said Amare, "but I'm not working for Whole fucking Pay Check."

You handed June a cigarette.

"Who said anything about you?" said Bill.

"How about a lighter?" she said.

Amare leaned back on his palms, letting the sun shine directly on his face, and closed his eyes. "You think that just because they offer organic produce and environmentally-friendly detergent that they're not an evil fucking corporate empire that exploits both their workers and the good intentions of hordes of guilt-ridden liberal douche bags? Not that I really give a fuck about those self-righteous idiots who think that they're doing anything other than aggravating their hemorrhoids by buying recycled toilet paper, but still."

Bill rolled his eyes. "Would you give it a rest? It's a grocery store."

Amare sat upright. "It's not a grocery store, dude. It's a monolithic corporate machine that sells organic foodstuffs. It bears no resemblance to the grocery stores of the past, where local owners bought and sold locally grown food."

"You're right," said Bill. "Those stores are in the past. But I don't live there. I live here, and here, at this time, in this universe in which I reside, I am unemployed. And anyway, better a monolithic corporation that sells recycled toilet paper than one that sells nothing but that ultra soft stuff they make from thousand year-old trees."

"I'll apply with you, Bill," said June.

Three heads pivoted as one.

She blushed. "What?"

You chuckled. Her eyes flashed like a pair of black volcanic rocks. "You think I couldn't do it?"

"I think you can do anything you want," you said.

Her features softened; she posed with straight-backed integrity. "Well I can."

"I've just never heard you express a desire to work at a grocery store before."

She dropped her half-smoked cigarette in the brown grass and crushed it with her sandal. "Who said this is about my desires? This is about getting a job so I can afford to get my own damn place."

You could only smile. While you felt you knew a few things about June's whims and resolve, it certainly wasn't in your best interest to say anything disparaging.

The two of you had moved in together too young and too soon. You'd been a twenty-three-year-old file clerk, hoping to break into the acting business; she'd been a twenty-year-old student at UCLA extension, taking a steadily diminishing number of classes per semester and working nights as a waitress at her mom's bikini bar—a shady establishment where young girls in skimpy bikinis danced on a stage while other girls in bikini tops and short shorts served drinks. Of course you wanted her to quit. Not because you couldn't stand the idea of lecherous drunks ogling her, or because the place was so unbearably seedy and dilapidated—in fact it was clean and bright, with some nice pool tables, streamers hanging from the ceiling, and a couple of bulky bouncers to make sure the clientele kept their hands to themselves—but primarily because of the mindfuck you imagined it did on her: doing that kind of work for her own mother. So, when you'd gotten a job as a bartender at an old Hollywood watering hole, you encouraged her to quit. Between your tips and the money that your dad was willing to kick down each month, you could swing her share of the rent. And quit she did. And for the first couple of weeks, your hopes were realized: June's mood improved, she applied herself to her schoolwork, she got encouraging feedback from her professors. But the extensions she asked for on her term papers quickly piled up, and, under the weight of concrete expectations, she crumbled. She ate less, drank more, watched TV until the sun came up and slept until it went down. She hardly acknowledged you when you came back from your shifts at the bar. For nearly a month you didn't have a civil conversation; any kind of inquiry about schoolwork was met with fury. Communication swung like a pendulum between screaming and silence.

At first her sister April's request to come live with you felt like a life raft—while April didn't have much money, every little bit helped, and surely June's behavior would change with a younger sibling around. And maybe things did get better for a couple of weeks; you couldn't remember. What you could remember was the shitstorm June unleashed the first time you stayed up late with April, smoking weed and talking photography. By the time you'd made it back to your room, June was curled up in bed in the fetal position, trembling. You'd immediately gone to her, felt her forehead, asked her if she was feeling okay. She exploded—accused you of trying to screw a teenager and threw a plate covered with two-day-old pizza crusts in the vicinity of your head. While the blast was contained to your room, the shockwaves reverberated throughout the apartment. April left early the next morning and didn't come home for three days and nights. Too furious to face June, you set up camp in the living room and slept on the couch. When April did return, both her and June acted like nothing had happened.

Then one day you arrived at work and your boss informed you that the rent on the bar had tripled and they were going to be laying off all recent hires. Just like that, you and June were both unemployed. It might not be fair to say that this development made her happy, but, on a dime, things shifted once again. Suddenly June was rubbing your shoulders, bringing you cold beer, and telling you it would all be okay, that you had each other and that together you would survive.

You tried to get another bartending gig, but, without knowing someone on the inside, bartending jobs resembled any other Hollywood cattle call audition—dozens of airbrushed hopefuls lined up outside some Sunset Boulevard meat market, trying desperately to project cool, competence, and sex appeal.

At more than one of these interviews, you were forced to pose for a Polaroid picture that they then stapled to your résumé. Rejection, fear, insecurity, and unemployment tucked you and June under a downy comforter of depression and together you fell away from the world. You survived on bagels, coffee, and cigarettes; you hemorrhaged cash on rent, bills, and a sufficient amount of bourbon to keep big feelings at bay; you sleepwalked through your home with the shades drawn, waiting for the executioner's axe to drop. When the blade came down the form of the eviction notice, you realized it wasn't at all the death blow you'd been fearing; what they'd actually handed you was a get-out-of-jail-free card. You wasted no time cashing it in.

*

GIVEN THE NUMBER OF bodies, the study room at the Homework Club was eerily quiet. Other than the hum of the air-conditioner, the scribbling of pencils, and the turning of textbook pages, the only voices you were treated to were the ones in your head. From the students came no chatter, gossip, snickering, or groaning. Four high school boys, obedient and respectful, all relatively new to the club, plodded through their biology, statistics, and calculus homework, not a single one of them yet grasping the upside of squandering an opportunity to lighten their workload. You weren't too confident in any of these subjects, so you read quietly, hoping that none of them would ask a question you couldn't answer—there was nothing you disdained more than having to suck humility and go to Tim and Eric for help.

These kids were part of the new breed. As much as Sophie frustrated you, she was at least a type that you were familiar

with. High school was changing. In the years since you'd
graduated, getting into a good college had become exponentially
tougher. The kinds of scores required just to be considered by
top universities forced these students to completely surrender
to the ambitions of their parents, teachers, and counselors. A
devout existentialist, this development troubled you. How was
the individual supposed to emerge when all these kids shared
the same goals? You had gone to a competitive prep school with
plenty of straight-A students, but straight As hadn't been the
norm. You had never felt defective for maintaining a B average.
You pursued subjects and activities that interested you. And yet
look at you now. Maybe you'd had it all wrong. Maybe the greatest
peril facing the young was the notion of individualism. You had
assumed that constraints and pressures placed on high school
students limited imaginations and hence, options. Maybe that
assumption was wrong. You had to concede that it was possible
that once set in motion, these kids might act without doubt and
thrive while you and your ilk mulled, pondered, procrastinated,
and dwelled.

At 5:30, the bell on the front door jingled. You swiveled in
your seat to see Sophie, half in the door, half out, facing the
street, her hip thrust toward the sidewalk like a baited hook.

"I cannn't!" she whined. "I need to do my geometry!"

You looked back at the studious assembly—faces emerging
from textbooks and huddled shoulders to look at one another
quizzically. An unintelligible voice responded to Sophie.

"Stop!" she said. "Don't be dirty."

Smiles tugged at the corners of the studious teenaged faces.
You stood up and walked to the door. Sophie sensed you and
held out an open palm, signaling for you to wait.

"Sophie," you said.

She thrust an index finger at you, indicating this would only take a second.

"Not until later!" she yelled. "My parents will be gone by eight."

"In or out?" you said.

"Huh?" said Sophie.

"That door is closing. I need you in or out."

"Just…ugh!" She went outside and the door swung closed. You resisted the urge to do exactly what she wanted you to do and ogle what you imagined was some quarterback hunk in the new BMW convertible his parents gave him for his sixteenth birthday. Your study-room students had lost interest and were again facedown in their textbooks. You didn't know where their powers of concentration came from, but you were somewhere between impressed and disturbed. *C'mon guys*, you thought. *A little bit of curiosity is a healthy thing.* Was she too predictable for them? Maybe these kids had already realized that pretty people call attention to themselves for the sole reason that they don't know who they are when no one is looking. Still, Sophie was a peer, and as a peer, they had a right to be intrigued by her shenanigans. Shouldn't they at least be shaking their heads or rolling their eyes in joint disapproval of the frivolity of it all? Now that you were thinking of it, their immersion in their studies was downright creepy. You wanted to yell: *Life is happening all around you, kids! I love to read too, but sometimes I learn more when I pick my head up. At some point you're going to need to know how to balance your social and academic lives. Practice. Now. Stop being such fucking nerds and engage a little bit. Ask me questions about girls, about life. Make me feel sage. Make me feel useful.*

The door opened and Sophie walked inside. Behind her was a well-built guy, about 5'9" with black-rimmed glasses, the strap from a canvas courier bag lashed diagonally across his chest like a seatbelt.

"Josh, this is Cameron."

"Hey," said Cameron, making brief, sheepish eye contact before finding a bookshelf to stare at.

"How's it going, man?" you said.

"Okay," he said. "She said to come inside. I don't know why."

"Cameron," she said, nestling up beside him and tucking her arms under his bicep. "Don't be like that. I told you I wanted to show you off."

"You lookin' for a place to study?" you said.

"I'm okay."

"How about a tutor?"

"No thanks, sir. Thanks though."

"Cameron's like a total genius," said Sophie.

"Oh yeah?"

Cameron shook his head. "I'm not a genius," he said. "I'm just good at school."

"What's the difference?" she said.

Cameron looked at you and shrugged as if to say, *There's some folks that if they don't already know, you can't tell 'em.*

"Is it okay if he stays here with me for a little while?" she said.

You sucked air through your closed teeth. "Soph, you know that's not really how we operate."

"C'mon Josh. His older sister is picking him up in a few minutes. And it's like a hundred bazillion degrees outside."

Cameron slipped out of Sophie's grasp and walked over to the bookshelf. He removed a book of Mary Oliver poems.

"You like her?" you said.

"She's my sister's favorite. I like her voice. It's clear. She's not trying to show off all the time, you know?"

"I agree," you said. "She's very clear."

"Some poets," he said, "when I read them, I feel like I'm picking through a junk pile, like if I examined each item, I could make sense of it, but it's not worth the effort."

Sophie beamed.

"He can stay," you said.

Cameron held up the book. "Mind if I read this?"

"Knock yourself out." You turned to Sophie. "How about we take a look at that geometry homework?"

"Thank you! Cameron tried to help me, but he kept going too fast. You move at the right pace, Josh. When you explain this stuff to me, I don't feel stupid."

"Aw," you said, feeling the red rush to your cheeks. "Thanks, Soph. But I have to say..."

"And you don't have to give any speeches today," she said. "I know I'm not stupid. It just feels that way when I keep making the same mistakes over and over again."

"No speeches," you said.

She smiled, dropped her heavy backpack on the table and took a seat.

*

THE MORNING ARRIVED THAT Bill and June had designated to go to Whole Foods for job applications, and June struggled to get out of bed. You weren't surprised; she'd been up and down all night. At three in the morning, you'd awoken to an orange glow leaking out from beneath the bathroom door. An hour or so later you'd gotten up to take a piss and discovered her still in the bathroom, sitting, in the dark, on the edge of the tub. She got up immediately, slipped wordlessly by and retreated, with your cigarettes, to the balcony. If she was trying to avoid you because she feared interrogation, there was something fundamental she was failing to grasp. Things had changed. Your adult life, while fluid and inchoate, was officially underway. You would no longer allow yourself to be lured into her well of worry. And besides, time spent apart had helped you recognize some things you'd previously been too close to see. Like the way nighttime transformed that well into a hole as depthless as it was dark. Given time to reflect, you could not recall, amongst countless sleepless hours, the illumination of a single, lasting resolution.

At some point in the late morning, you and Bill strolled to 7-Eleven for coffee. The oppressive heat had broken and, in the relative cool, rejuvenated trees stretched their limbs and straightened their trunks as if reemerging, unburdened, from productive therapy sessions. Light traffic breezed down the streets like the first fallen leaves of autumn. As you returned home, tendrils of steam escaping through the sip holes of your twenty-four-ounce French Roasts, you encountered an elderly couple, walking arm in arm. The man tipped his newsboy cap. You froze for a moment, startled by the old-world courtesy of the gesture.

"How you folks doing today?" said Bill.

"Just fine, young man," he said. "It's a beautiful day."

"It is, isn't it?" said Bill.

"That heat was just too much," said the woman.

"It wasn't civilized," said Bill.

The elderly couple smiled. "That's a funny way of putting it," said the woman, "but I suppose you're right. This weather, this is what we moved here for in the first place."

"I hear you," said Bill. "You folks enjoy it."

"Thank you!" The couple beamed as they walked past, as if, in exchanging platitudes, Bill had granted them temporary access to a world growing more and more elusive and incomprehensible.

"You practicing?" you said.

"Shut up."

"Hey, I don't blame you. Making conversation with strangers is hard. It's a muscle. You've got to exercise it."

"If I don't force myself be social, it gets so the simplest greeting can be a completely humiliating experience."

You patted him on the back. "You're like a big league pitcher, working his way back from injury."

He kicked at a pebble in his path but his shoe sailed clean over it. He chuckled mirthlessly. "I don't know. A farm-system rookie could charm a co-ed wearing a Coldplay tee shirt."

"C'mon now, man. That was a bad pairing. That's all. It's not like you didn't have the guts to be yourself."

"It's just that my 'self' was completely abhorrent to her."

"Always better to be honest."

"That how you snagged June?"

You sipped your too-hot coffee, scalding your tongue, and spit it onto the sidewalk. "Ouch. Fuck. I didn't… That's different."

"Because she's beautiful?"

"I don't know," you said. But you did know. You wiped your mouth and shook drops of French Roast from your hand. "I fucking hope not."

Bill touched your elbow. "You'd have no reason to be ashamed if it were."

"But I would. I would be deeply fucking ashamed."

"What can you do, man? Our values, the ones that define us, are mostly based on personal experience, right? They can't be based on experiences we haven't had yet. Out of the blue something or someone comes along that we never imagined or hadn't accounted for."

"In this case, a girl way hotter than I thought I could get."

"So you bend a little bit."

"You lie."

"To yourself…yeah. So that when you're lying to her, it's the truth according to the big lie."

"The big lie."

"The one you tell yourself."

He'd nailed you. In the only way that Bill could nail a person. Just speaking extemporaneously—no harm intended. And yet he'd unveiled something you'd never had the guts to recognize. You tried not to show it, took a cautious sip of coffee, nodded your head, sucked on your top teeth.

Your big lie had been that you were just being you. That was the reason you were better than those others—the ones who tried so hard to be what they thought she wanted. That you weren't trying anything—that was the big lie. Because underneath that confidence, you'd collected ample evidence that you weren't shit. That you were somehow defective. Why else would all the good ones have run for the hills the moment you'd expressed those big feelings of yours?

You were at the glass door to your building now, staring through it into the empty lobby. You dug your keys out of your pocket. "I think I hear what you're saying," you said. "You're saying that the trick to avoiding ulcers is believing your own bullshit."

"As far as I know, that's the trick to everything, from getting a girl to getting a job to buying a new sweater at The Gap."

You laughed.

"Seriously." Bill patted his chest. "What right do I have to waltz into The Gap and buy a new sweater? I've got plenty of clothing. I don't need that sweater. I certainly don't deserve that sweater. I should buy that sweater and take it directly to some homeless guy on the street. But I don't because I've lied to myself. I've told myself: 'I need this' or 'I deserve this.' It's bullshit."

"Bill," you said, holding open the door. "There's nothing that you can imagine for yourself that you don't deserve."

Bill smiled. "Yeah, well. Right now my imagination is the exclusive domain of Pedro Martinez. At least until baseball season's over."

You laughed, pretending that the comment didn't make you just a little sad.

Back in the apartment, you headed straight for the balcony. That word—*imagination*—had been stirring your guts since the moment you'd said it. Even more so because it seemed to be gaining prominence in your functional vocabulary. You'd said something to Julia—that being a tutor wasn't what you'd imagined yourself becoming. You'd dropped that statement so casually, like letting go of the future you'd imagined for yourself had been equivalent to letting go of a toy that hadn't held your attention since childhood. Like it wasn't a big deal that your indecisions were just as potent as your decisions.

There had been a time when imagination was all you were— and it's not as if you hadn't tried to align it with reality. You'd kept acting after college, joining a scene-study group and honing your craft. You'd tried to get an agent. But a couple of *no*s went a long way toward undermining your confidence. Then there was that time you'd paid four hundred dollars to that service that advertised an 80 percent success rate in gaining representation for aspiring actors. They'd identify which agencies might be interested in someone like you, address all the envelopes, and help you craft a cover letter. When they'd done their job, you and your parents made piles on the living room floor and stuffed two hundred headshots—one smoldering, one sweet—into a hundred envelopes along with a cover letter containing words like *irreverent* and *sardonic* that you were certain would make you stand out from the pack. A hundred agencies responded with absolute silence.

You tried to shake it off, blame the service, blame your own credulity; you reminded yourself that getting started was hard work. But that silence had crushed something deep within, something you failed to rebuild. Recently, during an idle moment at The Homework Club, you'd read that astronomers had discovered sound waves coming from a massive black hole 250 million light years from earth. They'd detected a note—a B-flat, playing fifty-seven octaves lower than middle C. You'd wanted to invite the astronomers to point their equipment at Hollywood, see if B-flat was the precise pitch at which the industry smothered a billion cries of *love me*.

*

YOU NAVIGATED THE WHOLE Foods parking lot with caution; sparkling Lexuses and hulking Escalades circled like hawks, their owners frantic to return to vacant work stations or little children, left in the charge of the some matronly, woefully underpaid housekeeper. Amare denounced the drivers as either yuppie, fascist, or liberal scum depending upon their vehicle's miles per gallon. Your car, a mid-nineties Toyota Corolla that got about twenty miles per gallon, was exempt from judgment.

One of the benefits of a sub-middling income was that of accountability: your choices were a reflection of your bankroll, not your ethics.

Your gaze lingered longingly on a brand new midnight-blue Prius with a bumper sticker stating *Let Us Not Become The Evil We Deplore*. The sentiment seemed beyond even Amare's reproach. You couldn't help pointing it out.

He grunted. "Too late for that."

You swerved your car into an empty spot. "Yeah, well, better that than *Support Our Troops*."

"Some of those people have relatives over there," said Bill.

Amare unbuckled his seatbelt and stared out the rear window. "That doesn't mean they're not missing the point."

June, still half asleep and all but invisible during the ride over, faced the backseat.

"The point," said Bill, "is that they want their loved ones, who are risking getting blown to a million fregging pieces, to feel supported if they make it home."

"I completely disagree with that," countered Amare. "A *Support Our Troops* bumper sticker is purely antagonistic. It challenges anyone who knows better to point out that this war is bullshit."

"My brother is in Iraq," said June.

Amare didn't blink. "Shit. That sucks for him."

"His pool cleaning business went under. The Army said his tour would only be a year. His wife and kid would get health care and everything."

"How long has he been there?"

"Four months."

"Sometimes I think I should just go back to Providence," said Bill, "live with my parents and wait for the world to end."

"That's stupid," you said, preferring to address Bill's fatalism to June's brother's situation. June's brother was the first person from your generation that you'd known to go to war. When you and June had been a real couple, you'd seen him with some frequency. The two of you had gotten along well, shot hoops at the park down the street from his apartment; he'd even been your guest a couple of times at the Wednesday night pick-up game. It embarrassed you that June had withheld something so big.

"You're not moving home and the world's not going to end. Not today. Today we're picking up some job applications. That's it. Let's not make the little things harder than they need to be."

"I don't know if I can stomach this," said Amare.

"No one asked you to come in," said Bill. "I don't want you coming in there with us if you're gonna shit all over everything."

Amare scratched his stubbly cheek; translucent flakes of skin, illuminated by the sunlight, floated through the stuffy air. "They got a salad bar?"

"It's good," you said brightly. "They've got marinated artichokes, roasted bell peppers, beets."

"My colon could sure use a scraping," he said. "But I'm not paying ten bucks for a fucking salad though, if that's what it costs."

"Christ!" said Bill. He got out of the car, slammed the door and headed toward the entrance. June, taking up as little room as possible in the passenger seat, picked her ravaged nails, the only visible physical manifestation, other than the slight discoloration beneath her left eye, of a life in turmoil.

"You ready?" you said.

She exhaled. "So I'm supposed to go in there and beg some girl you used to sleep with for a job, is that the idea?"

A surge of electric current passed through your veins. You wrung the steering wheel like a boa constrictor squeezing the last drop of life from a mouse. June was surgical. No one could open you up and prick your nerves faster or more efficiently. Now you had to flee. Anything said in anger would be filed away for later, exhumed when she needed evidence of your cruelty. You opened the car door but didn't move from your seat. You opened your mouth to speak but found no words.

"I'll stay with you, June," said Amare. Your mouth snapped shut in surprise. The two of them rarely engaged in direct conversation; Bill was the conduit through which June and the boys communicated. In fact, you weren't certain you'd ever heard Amare say her name.

She looked up from her nails, caught his reflection in the rear view mirror. "You will?"

"This place looks like a fucking nightmare."

"Didn't you have Whole Foods in Olympia?" she said.

"Sure, but I got my groceries at work...the Olympia Food Co-op. None of this corporate bullshit."

"Olympia sounds cool."

"Olympia's a shithole," said Amare.

"Really?"

"It rained for ninety-three straight days my sophomore year. Don't get me wrong, if black mold, 6:00 a.m. happy hours, and chronic bronchitis are qualities you're looking for in a city, it could be the place for you."

You and June laughed. You stepped out of the car and tossed the keys onto the driver's seat. "In case you want the radio," you said.

"You've gotta get satellite radio," said Amare. "They were playing Mitch Hedberg on the comedy station a few weeks ago. *Mitch Hedberg.*"

"Awesome," you said.

"It's like ten bucks a month."

"Okay."

"You live in Los Angeles! You drive everywhere! This is a good investment! For ten bucks a month you could dramatically improve your life!"

"I said I'll think about it! Jesus!" Amare shrugged. You closed the car door and headed toward the entrance, where Bill was shuffling his feet, adrift amongst the summer flower bouquets.

"Do I look like a thief?" he said.

"What?"

He motioned toward an employee, engaged in the act of sweeping. "I swear this guy over here thinks I'm trying to steal something. He asked me if I needed any help twice already and now he's sweeping an area that we can all plainly see is spotless. Watch him for two seconds; tell me if I'm nuts."

"I don't have to wait two seconds to tell you that."

"There!" he said. "You see that?"

"That guy can suck a bag of dicks." You put your arm around his shoulders and led him through the sliding doors. Bill glanced back, and as you entered the market, he nearly tripped over a toddler clinging to her mother's hand.

"Oh shit," he said. "I'm so sorry."

"Shit," said the little blonde girl with shiny red butterfly bonnets in her hair. "Oh shit, oh shit."

The mother's face contorted into an ugly frown. "Great," she said. "That's just wonderful."

"I said I was sorry," said Bill.

She tugged her daughter towards the parking lot.

"Oh shit!" called the little girl.

"Shake it off, big guy," you said. "I think I just spotted our girl."

Bill faced the interior of the market and froze. He scanned from left to right, taking in the deli counter and its neighboring olive bar, the racks of premium wine, two aisles devoted entirely to herbal supplements and homeopathic remedies, a towering display of puffed corn and rice snacks, and off to the right, heaps of fresh produce, glistening beneath a shower of mist.

"I'm still adjusting to this city," he said. "So much of it looks like a movie set."

"I know what you mean," you said. "But Whole Foods is Whole Foods. Go into a Whole Foods in Bumfuck, Idaho, and I imagine it would look exactly like this."

"You've clearly never been to Idaho"

You shrugged. "Why do you say that?"

Bill nodded towards a tall brunette wearing black tights and a pink form-fitting sweatshirt. "Because no one who looks like *that* lives there."

You found your girl in the produce section, doing some kind of inventory of the softball-sized yellow onions.

"Sadie," you said.

She looked at you and her eyes widened in immediate recognition. "Josh!" she said as she moved in and hugged you. She stepped back, her fingertips still touching your elbows. "Holy shit, dude! What's up?"

She'd put on a few pounds but they were the good kind, the kind of pounds that implied health and happiness. You were deeply embarrassed, and not because you'd invaded her privacy or altered a perception of a memory that somehow gave your life a narrative; you were embarrassed by the fact that you'd ever gone out of your way to avoid such a kindhearted person. While real human warmth and contact were being replaced by an exploding digital ethos, here was Sadie, hugging and kissing you.

"It's great to see you too," you said. "You look fantastic."

She rolled her eyes. "Shit. I've been up since five this morning. I'm totally fried." She spied Bill hovering behind your shoulder. "Who's your friend?"

"Bill, meet Sadie. Sadie, Bill."

"Great to meet you," said Bill, emerging from behind you with excellent posture, taking her hand in his, shaking it firmly and carefully maintaining eye contact.

"You from LA?" she said.

"Nope. Only been here a few weeks." Bill stuffed his hands in his pockets but managed to avoid looking at the ground. He'd been struck by the slightly dumb smile that you'd always worn in the presence of Sadie—the easy, relieved smile of a person liberated from the fear of making a poor impression, a smile that accompanies the hunch that just about anything you say will be responded to with sincere interest.

"I went to college in Washington State. I never thought I'd end up in LA, but I knew a few people down here who were all super cool so…"

"Might as well give the sunshine a chance, right?"

"That's about the size of it, yeah."

Sadie rubbed her chin between her thumb and forefinger. "I had a friend who went to school in Olympia, Washington. A little hippie school called Evergreen where no one got grades and you designed your own major."

"That's my school!" said Bill. "That's where I went!"

"Awesome!" said Sadie. "I loved Olympia! I loved the rain and the bars and the music and the coffee shops. And Mount Rainier! What's more beautiful than Mount Rainier?"

Bill smiled. "It's true," he said to you.

You laughed. "I've seen it."

Sadie said, "I loved that no matter where I was in the city, when I looked out the window, there it was."

"Yeah," said Bill. "You know...I loved that too."

Sadie sighed and stared off behind us like Mount Rainer was there in plain sight, clear as day. Then something or someone intercepted her vision and suddenly she was back.

"David!" she called out. "Hey guys, it's been really nice seeing and meeting you, but I gotta get back to work. We should totally hang out though!" she said, squeezing your wrist.

"I'd love to," you and Bill said simultaneously.

Sadie beamed. You couldn't believe that you'd ever gone out of your way to avoid seeing this person. What a fool.

"Come here," she said, and gave each of you a parting hug.

You and Bill floated towards the exits and were just passing the registers when it struck both of you that you'd forgotten what you'd come for. Bill doubled back, assuring you he'd be fine and returned a minute later with an application.

"Got it!" he said, holding it up like a golden ticket. "She said they're interviewing a whole slew of applicants in a week!"

"Terrific," you said.

"I can't believe my luck!"

"Let's not get ahead of ourselves," you said.

"What? You think I won't get it?"

"I think you've got as good a shot as anyone else."

"I've got Sadie on my side," he said. "She winked at me when she told me about the opening."

"Yeah, well. I'm not sure the decision is hers, is all."

Bill's face fell. He looked down at the single sheet of paper, so flimsy and yet so imbued with possibility.

"Fuck," you said. You put your hand on his shoulder. "I don't mean to discourage you. I'm sure having Sadie on your side can't hurt your chances."

"She's like the nicest person I've ever met."

"Yeah," you said. "That's about the size of it."

*

HAVING FOREGONE THE WHOLE Foods salad bar, the boys went for chili burgers at Jack's. With the apartment quiet and a free hour before you had to leave for work, you pulled Ray Carver's *Where I'm Calling From* off the shelf and opened it to one of a hundred or so dog-eared pages. The idea of starting something new, like the idea of going to gym when you were out of shape, made you weary. You needed something you could slip into with ease, a voice to which your ear was already attuned.

A few pages in, you heard a sigh and the moan of mattress springs, as June made her way to the bathroom and switched on the ceiling fan. Bathroom door ajar, the faucet ran in the shower/tub, water tumbling down the drain. You tried to focus, to stay with the story—a favorite of yours about a father and son and the protective violence that lurks beneath love's surface—but the sound of June's brush, working out the knots in her hair in preparation for a shower, severed your connection to the words. While June had been sleeping in your bed for a couple of weeks now, there'd been no sex. The temptation had caused some restless nights, but her precarious emotional state, coupled with Bill and Amare's presence on the other side of a curtain, had stopped you from acting out your carnal impulses. You closed Carver and walked to the kitchen table to retrieve your cigarettes, planning to wait out her shower on the balcony, but your head turned just long enough to glimpse her reflection in the mirror—naked, her dark brown hair hanging down just past her waist. She caught you looking, bumped the door with her hip, but when it didn't close all the way, she made no further effort to shut it. You returned to the couch and tried to dive back into your reading but it was too late. You chain-locked the front door and stood outside the bathroom, breathing heavily. You knocked; she opened the door wide, leaving nothing to the imagination. And then it happened, up against the slick bathroom wall with your pants around your ankles, steam curling around your writhing bodies like a snake.

Afterward, sharing a shower like the old days, you said, "I'm gonna be out late tonight. Grabbing a drink with Harrison after work."

She stopped rinsing conditioner from her hair to adjust the shower head setting. "The fuck is with your water pressure?"

"What do you mean? It was a total selling point when I rented this place."

"I'm spoiled I guess," she said. "Dean's shower was crazy. It had two shower heads and each one had six settings."

"That's spectacular," you said, stepping out, sopping wet, onto the bathmat.

She continued to rinse her hair long after the last soap sparkle had dissolved. She was still in the bathroom when, a short while later, you left for work.

*

ANOTHER ADRIENNE-LESS EVENING PASSED at The Homework
Club after which you pointed your car in the direction of The
Burrow. It was Thursday night; with the Homework Club closed
for business on Fridays, the first night of your weekend. You'd
expected to hear from Harrison days ago—it had been over a
week since he took the LSATs—but until this morning, he'd
joined Adrienne on the AWOL list. Apparently, he'd stayed
on at the motel. Your curiosity was piqued. Once that test was
out of the way, you'd expected the kind of celebration that
would prevent you from being able to drive home, require you
to sleep it off at the motel rather than risk a DUI. But on the
phone, Harrison's voice sounded raspy and weak, as if he hadn't
used his vocal chords for days. Absent was the timbre of the
recently liberated.

As you neared Los Feliz, you succumbed to guilt and duty,
took the off ramp at Cahuenga Boulevard and made a detour
toward your parents' house. You'd gotten off work early and you
stank neither of cigarette smoke nor torpidity, so this seemed
like as good a time as any to make an appearance. If you were
going to continue concealing June's presence at your apartment,
it was best to show up when you'd been physically separated for
a few hours, when the weight of her world wasn't placed quite
so squarely on your shoulders. By this point in time, your folks
had developed a sixth sense; to them, the particular brand of
melancholia with which she infected you was as apparent as a
head cold.

Dusk fell as you navigated your car up the serpentine
circulatory system of the Hollywood Hills, centrifugal force
careening your basketball around the trunk. At a stop sign,
a skunk tumbled out of the ivy carpet that ran alongside the
road and sniffed around in the gutter. Its black eyes glinted in

your headlights and it raised its tail but the threat proved to be empty, as the critter assessed your car's bulk and retreated back into the tangled thicket from whence it came.

The brand new net on the basketball hoop in your parent's driveway gleamed in the motion-sensor lights triggered by your arrival. You texted Harrison, saying you'd be another hour, got out of the car and put one foot in front of the other. The front door opened and there was your mom, smiling hugely at her grown boy. Her hair was shorter than the last time you'd seen her and possibly a different color, more auburn than brown; you could see in her face that she'd dropped a few pounds.

"Josh!" She stepped through the threshold and hugged you. Her hand went to the small of your back, guided you through the doorway, and she called down the hall. "Ed! Josh is here!"

"You look good, Mom."

She rubbed your back and smiled. "Thank you!" She touched your chin and examined your face. "You look tired."

"Sorry to show up like this without calling. I just got off work."

"What time is it?" She leaned back and peered through squinted eyes at the living room clock. "Oh my, is it after eight already?" She frowned. You followed her into the kitchen. "There's leftover chicken piccata," she said, removing a Tupperware container from the fridge. "I can make a salad."

You got in between her and the fridge, retrieved a bag of romaine lettuce from the crisper. "I can do it."

"How about a glass of wine?"

You emptied the contents of the bag into the salad spinner. "No, thank you," you said. "Water's fine."

"Hey!" your dad appeared in the kitchen wearing a white tee shirt and pleated khakis, a folded *Sports Illustrated* tucked in his armpit. He tossed the magazine onto the counter, waited for you to finish rinsing the lettuce and gave you a hug. He patted your cheek with an open palm. "Good to see you, sweetheart."

"Dad," you grumbled.

He raised his palms. "Sorry, sorry."

"I'm in my mid-twenties. I'm going bald for chrissakes."

"Nonsense. Your hair looks great. That Propecia is really working." His eyebrows climbed his forehead. "You see what Pedro did tonight?"

"I just got off work."

"Eight innings, two hits, ten Ks. They all say Halladay's gonna win the Cy Young because of the complete games, but give me a healthy Pedro any day."

Your mom covered a plate of chicken with a sheet of wax paper and stuck it in the microwave. "How's your week going?"

You shrugged. "My favorite student hasn't been around lately. I miss her."

"Is this the one you told me about? With the green hair?"

"Adrienne, yeah." You pulled the chord on the salad spinner a few times and let it whirl. "I feel a little unnecessary when she's not there. Like my particular skill set isn't doing anyone any good."

"Nonsense," said Dad, as he sat down at the table. "They'd be lost without you."

You snorted. "How could you possibly know that?"

"I know how smart you are and I know how good you are with kids. What else do I need to know?"

You swallowed your objections and tore lettuce leaves into edible pieces. The microwave hummed. "Mom," you said. "You shouldn't stand so close."

"Oh." She stepped away. "I should watch that, shouldn't I?" She opened the cupboard and began setting the table for one.

Your dad cleared some phlegm from his throat. "And how are your...your buddies back there?"

He couldn't be faulted for having failed to commit Bill and Amare's names to memory. While your folks had known of them for a while, they'd never actually met. As you searched for an answer, a vision of the scene at the apartment popped into your head: Bill sprawled across whatever floor space availed itself, nagging Amare to change the channel to the MLB Network so he could get a Red Sox score, his blank Whole Foods application sitting on the counter, waiting to be completed or lost; Amare lounging on the couch, hunting for news—any news would do—that would support his worldview; June hunched before the computer, scouring the internet for jobs that she'd never apply for and pick-picking away at those nails of hers—the three of them waiting around for the pizza delivery guy or the apocalypse, whichever should happen to arrive first.

"Bill's applying for a job."

Your mom sighed. "I still can't believe that that tiny room can sleep all three of you."

You sat down at the table with your salad. "It's not so tiny."

She shrugged. "Not for one person maybe."

You spoke through a mouthful of lettuce. "It's temporary."

The phone rang. Your dad kept talking as he wandered off down the hall to answer it. "You should have 'em over here for dinner. I've got more steaks in the freezer than I'll ever eat."

"I thought you were off red meat for awhile," you yelled. You looked at mom. "The IBS getting better?"

She rolled her eyes. "There was a sale at Gelson's. He couldn't help himself."

Dad walked back into the kitchen, clutching the cordless phone like a baseball that had just crashed through his window.

"Another one of those goddamned telemarketers. I can tell from the number."

Mom smiled wearily. "You don't have to answer it."

"It's after eight."

"Dad," you said. "Mom says you cleaned out Gelson's."

"Prime cut steaks at half price, Josh. The good stuff." His eyes twinkled.

You laughed. "But you can't eat them."

"So bring the boys over for dinner. I can live vicariously."

Even nuked, the chicken piccata was delicious, like all your mom's cooking. You had to be mindful not to scarf, to chew every bite, answer their questions, ask some of your own; you didn't want them getting the impression that you weren't eating enough. One hint at deprivation and they'd start showing up at your apartment with enough cold cuts and and potato salad to feed the entire complex.

After you finished, your dad suggested that you stick around for a while, watch some Sox highlights, but you didn't want to keep Harrison waiting any longer. You said your goodbyes and your mom accompanied you to the gate. As you backed out of a hug, a gentle but firm hand grasped your arm.

"What's the plan tonight?" she said.

"No real plans. Just a bar."

She let go and crossed her arms over her chest. "I've never really understood that—how people can drive to a bar, drink for a while and then drive home. You don't drive drunk, do you?"

You shook your head emphatically. "We just talk and have a few rounds. We don't drink to excess."

"It would take me hours to sober up from a few rounds."

You smiled. "Just two or three beers. We're big boys. We can handle it."

She frowned.

"Don't you trust me to make good decisions?"

She looked you right in the eyes and half smiled.

"Everything okay, Mom?"

She rubbed her arms as though she were cold, breathed in and out. "I just want you to know that you can talk to me. That's all. If there's anything at all that you're struggling with."

That falling sensation triggered by a close brush with the truth raced through your belly. You hugged her—the best way to hide what whatever story your face might betray. "I know that, Mom." You held on for an extra beat. Years of acting workshops were useless against her compassion. "Everything's good." You stepped back and held her by the shoulders. You let her see your eyes. "I'm just tired. Those kids take a lot out of me."

She half smiled and half winced, perhaps sensing the deceit lurking behind your platitudes.

"I'll come back soon. I promise. I'll bring the boys."

"When is soon?"

"I'll call tomorrow when I've got my calendar in front of me."

That seemed to satisfy her. She nodded and kissed your cheek. She stood by the gate and watched as you pulled out of the driveway.

*

NIGHTTIME HAD FALLEN BY the time you arrived at the bar, but the sun had set on the The Burrow years ago. The feeble light that seeped through the stained glass windows betrayed no hint as to the time of day; its provenance could just as easily be in a streetlight or noonday sunshine. Half a dozen moribund regulars huddled over their drinks, rooting through the remnants of ravaged popcorn bags and gazing at the Dodgers game on the muted television set. You happily took your seat amongst them. The door hinge squeaked behind you and before you knew it, Harrison was standing at your side, squinting at the television. He smelled strongly of cigarettes.

"Jesus, man," you said. "You look like hell."

He unbuttoned the collar of his wrinkled white shirt. His sunken cheeks had grown a sparse layer of facial hair—he never really could grow a full beard, but his scruff lent him the appearance of a pseudo-intellectual movie star, trying to look like he wasn't trying.

"Yeah," he said, scratching his neck. "I don't know what to tell ya. I was expecting I'd want to celebrate, blow off some steam as soon as it was over. Then…I don't know."

"How about I buy you a shot and a beer and you tell me about it?" You raised your hand, trying to get Leanne's attention. Entranced by the game, she didn't see you.

Harrison sat down as you leaned forward, trying to insert yourself into Leanne's peripheral vision. He said, "When I was in elementary school, I was the best basketball player in my class."

"I've heard the stories," you said. "Leanne?"

"But by sixth grade, my run was almost over. There was this other kid, Mikai. He was always shorter than I was, but that year, he grew like five inches and his game kept improving too. One day he'd show up with a crossover, the next he'd have a finger-roll, and all the while his muscles were developing so that he metamorphosed from a chubby kid into this young Adonis. Finally, he decided he'd heard enough of my talk and, at lunchtime, he challenged me to a game of one-on-one."

Behind the cloudiness of his eyes, something glimmered with the vitality of a fresh idea.

"I could shoot, but in a game of one-on-one, I knew Mikai would just blow by me every time. And we were playing buckets, so there was a chance I might never see the ball. But it had been drizzling all morning. The court was wet. I figured the slick surface would negate some of his quickness. Plus, a bunch of kids heard the challenge and they were all razzing me, and I had my rep to protect. Conditions being what they were, I figured I wasn't going to get a better shot, so I agreed."

"And you got slaughtered and learned an important lesson in humility?"

"No."

"I was kidding."

Harrison's gaze landed on the mirror and his lips turned up in a perceptibly private grin, as though he'd discovered, in his pallid reflection, the punch line to an inside joke.

"I caught fire. Beat him eleven-to-one. All the kids were chanting my name."

"How many kids are we talking about?"

"I don't know. In my mind, it's at least fifty, and they were yelling and high-fiving, and I might be conflating this bit with *Rudy*, but I'm pretty sure I got carried off the blacktop on their shoulders."

You laughed. "You learned an important lesson in your own greatness."

"You're wrong." He held up his index finger. "That one point that Mikai scored, I don't know how he got traction on that court, but he did, and he blew by me like I was nailed to the fucking ground. The next play, he slipped in a puddle, lost the handle and the ball went of bounds. I stood there at the top of the key, holding the ball in my hands, knowing that I had to make every shot or it was over. I was toast. It's crazy. A year before, it wouldn't have been a contest. I would've trounced him. But those days were over. He was better than me. And yeah, I won that day, I played the best I possibly could, but I refused to ever play one-on-one with Mikai again."

"But you were a better shooter."

"Not for long, I wasn't. Look, I wasn't Magic Johnson; I didn't have a single-minded obsession; I didn't shoot baskets for hours after school every day, rain or shine. I knew that in order to keep on beating Mikai, I'd have to work as tirelessly on my weaknesses as he worked on his. That day was one of my greatest individual sports moments, but in that moment I recognized that there's a ceiling on natural ability, and that the people who ultimately succeed are the ones that aren't scared to confront their weaknesses, they're the ones who work on them every fucking day until they transform those weaknesses into strengths. These people aren't paralyzed by the fear that they're making the wrong choices and they're not plagued by anxiety about all the other shit they're missing out on."

"What happened to you this week?"

He sighed. "I let go of my doubts."

"Okay?"

His misty eyes roamed the scenery as if he were examining each detail of the room, trying to match things up with a mental image fixed in his memory.

"I was in the zone. I stopped questioning whether being a lawyer was something I really wanted. After the test was over, I assessed my weaknesses and kept on working."

"In your motel room?"

"Yep."

"Hunkered down, twenty-four-seven."

"I left to resupply a couple times. You know, pick up coffee, Captain Crunch, bananas, milk, cigarettes. The essentials."

You put a hand on his shoulder. "I'm pretty sure that qualifies as a some kind of breakdown."

He laughed. "I know I need a real meal," he said, "but I'm not hungry. That's why I agreed to meet you here. I figured a few drinks might improve my appetite."

Something happened in the Dodgers game and the bar's patrons started grumbling to one another.

You squeezed the back of his neck. "There's more to an application than a test score."

"Man, fuck that test!"

A few of the regulars turned their heads.

"I don't get it."

"Josh, listen to what I'm saying: the test is moot. If I can keep going like this, no fucking thing they can throw at me can slow me down."

Leanne leaned on the bar, showing Harrison her cleavage. "I haven't see you in a while," she said. "What you like?"

"Bourbon," he said. "Double."

"I'm listening," you said. "Please expound. I'll start: this week, I found god in a law book."

He chuckled. "Now we're talkin."

You sipped your beer. "Can I get a bourbon too please, Leanne?"

Leanne nodded without diverting her gaze from her task. She put a glass of bourbon in front of him. "Thank you, darling." Harrison cupped it in his hands. "I fucked off a lot in school. You know, you were there. I took it just seriously enough to pull good grades. But I had no idea what I was going to do after it was over, so I didn't feel like I was working toward anything meaningful. I wanted the grades because I wanted to graduate cum laude. I wanted to feed my ego."

"There's nothing wrong with letting vanity motivate you. As long as what it's motivating you to do doesn't hurt anybody."

"That's a very fucking Josh thing to say." He sipped his bourbon and winced. "Jesus, this is awful. Leanne?" Leanne hustled over and leaned in, again proffering that rack of hers. Harrison was oblivious. "I want to know what this is so I never order it again."

"Just in the well. It's…" she bent over and read the label. "Kessler's," she said.

"Leanne, no more Kessler's. We're grown men. Time to drink from the grown man shelf."

"Jim Beam?" you said.

"Not good enough," said Harrison. "What's a nice bourbon, Leanne?"

"We have Baker's," she said, retrieving it from the top shelf. "Very nice. Very expensive."

"Two Baker's," said Harrison.

"What's happening here?" you said. "What kind of drink is this?"

Harrison winked. Leanne placed the bourbons on the bar.

"Eighteen dollar," she said.

Harrison put twenty-five dollars on the bar and told Leanne to keep the change. You marveled at her instincts. At first glance, the only difference in Harrison had been his level of dishevelment and emaciation, yet somehow Leanne had sensed a change more fundamental than his appearance from the moment he'd walked in the door, and it seemed she'd intuited that it was going to benefit her financially.

Harrison sipped the bourbon, reverently set the glass on the bar and sighed like he'd just slipped into a hot bath at the end of a long day. "That's the stuff, Leanne," he said. "From now on, when I walk in that door, I want a glass of Baker's waiting for me on the bar."

Leanne laughed and swept her hair off her shoulder.

"I feel like we're celebrating your release from prison."

"Prison?"

"Like you've emerged from some kind of cerebral vortex, a self-imposed punishment for not taking your life seriously enough."

Harrison sang, "I've got freedom, freedom, freedom... freedom if nothing else. Nearly time to go, and I still don't know, what freedom means myself." He smiled hugely and swallowed the rest of his bourbon. "Drink that. It's good for you."

You swallowed the bourbon in one shot. Its warmth radiated from your belly to your chest.

"Nurse!" he cried. "Medication please!" He slapped twenty-five more dollars on the bar.

You put your hand on his forearm. "How 'bout we put some food in our bellies before we go down this road?"

He grabbed your arm. The whites of his eyes were red and cloudy but his irises gleamed like sunlight passed through a magnifying glass. "Sometimes a man comes to a point where he says, 'I'm doing this now, and nothing else matters because what I'm doing makes sense.' "I know myself here. I look in the mirror and don't feel like there's a stranger is staring back at me." He took a deep breath and let it out. His eyes brimmed with tears. The bar was quiet, as though each patron was discreetly listening, hanging on his every word. "My parents are good people. They raised me better than to spend so much energy hating myself."

He stopped and stared into his refilled bourbon glass like he was looking over the edge of a tall building.

"Your parents live in this world too," you said. "There's nothing you've been feeling that they haven't felt themselves. They just hid it from you is all. For the same reasons you'll hide it from your kids."

Harrison nodded. He held his bourbon up to the light and admired it. "To cutting ourselves a break."

You clinked your glasses together and sipped your grown-man drinks.

Harrison didn't have enough cash to buy a third round, but Leanne's generous pours had more than done the trick. You left The Burrow and stumbled down Los Feliz Boulevard. A few smokers loitered outside Barfly, a soulless, trendy meat market, with watered down drinks, seven-dollar beers and a huge portrait of Mickey Rourke playing the role of Charles Bukowski.

Harrison stopped, squinted at the doorman wearing a grey tank top and said, "It's a little breezy tonight, homie. That sucks that they don't let you wear sleeves."

The doorman looked confused. "What are you talking about?"

"You know...for warmth."

The doorman scratched his chin. "Do I know you?"

Harrison threw up his arms. "I'm the ghost of Hank fucking Chinaski!"

"You're a loser."

"Says the doorman." Harrison elbowed your ribs and cackled.

The doorman stood up from his stool. "The fuck did you just say, loser?"

"Nothing, man." Harrison resumed his stumble down the sidewalk, but couldn't resist a parting shot. "I just stated a fact. That you're a doorman."

"Just keep on walking, loser," called the doorman.

But Harrison wasn't listening. He was humming a Grateful Dead tune and fumbling with his cigarette lighter. As you passed a throng of smokers, a skinny brunette wearing a mini-skirt and platform sandals turned to her friend and said, "Who's Hank Chinaski?"

Her friend crushed the butt of her cigarette with her high heels. "Who cares?"

You moaned. "Bukowski is rolling over in his grave."

Harrison chuckled, looked back over his shoulder and ogled the girls. "No he ain't."

You bought a six-pack and half a dozen tacos and went back to Harrison's motel. The air in his room was rancid with cigarette butts and sour milk. A flickering neon light trickled through diaphanous curtains, illuminating a half-eaten bowl of soggy, coagulated cereal; books blanketed the unmade bed. How he had gotten his hands on so many ashtrays you didn't know, but they overflowed on every available surface.

While Harrison scarfed down tacos, you cracked a beer and called the apartment. It rang four times and the machine picked up. You hung up and dialed again. This time Amare picked up on the first ring.

"Hello?"

"Hey man, it's Josh."

"Yo."

"Everything okay over there?"

"What do you mean?"

"What are you guys up to?"

"Nothing. Bill got drunk and passed out."

"He did?"

"And June left."

"She what?"

"You should pick up some beer on the way home. Bill drank whatever was left in the fridge."

You retreated to the bathroom and closed the door. "How long ago did she leave?"

"I don't know. Half an hour. She took her bag."

"Did she say where she was going?"

"Nope. She was on the balcony for a while, talking on her phone. Then she got her giant bag and walked out without saying a word."

"Fuck me."

There was a knock on the door. "Gotta pee," called Harrison.

"One sec," you said.

"You comin' home tonight?" said Amare.

"I don't know."

"Got. Ta. Pee."

"Well, don't forget the beer. I mean, if you want any."

"Right."

You hung up, flushed the toilet and splashed some water on your face. You opened the door to find Harrison, leaning against the wall beside the door, a burning cigarette between his lips.

"Fucking whatdoyoucallit." He snapped his fingers a few times. "Lancet liver fluke!"

He didn't make way so you lowered your shoulder and bumped past him. You pushed aside a mound of books and sat down on the bed.

"June left?" he said.

"I don't know. Maybe."

"Glory hallelujah."

"Sooner or later she'll waltz back through the door like nothing ever happened."

"Not if you don't let her."

You closed your phone, flipped it open and closed it again. "I can't do that. Not now."

Harrison stood there for a minute, staring right through you. He shook his head back and forth and clicked his tongue disapprovingly.

"You're better than that, Josh."

"She's sleeping in my bed."

"Man…you fucking fucked her!"

"I thought you had to piss."

He kept staring for a few seconds, then turned and crashed into the unlit bathroom. You heard him struggle with his belt, then the torrential downpour of alcoholic piss. "You fucked yourself, homie," he yelled. "Fucked yourself good."

You straightened up, put some volume behind your voice. "What changed tonight?"

"What do you mean?"

"Why come out of your room *tonight*? Why stop whatever it was you were doing?"

His piss turned from deluge to light sprinkle; it was followed by a zip and a flush. He emerged from the bathroom and made his way over to the beer. "All work and no play, I guess."

You stood and parted the threadbare curtains. The street, draped by a pale sheet of moonlight, looked empty and indifferent, as if the cool night wind had erased all memory of the daily car crashes and traffic jams waged on its stained and mottled surface.

"I think too much," you said.

"Of course you do, man. That's your thing."

"It's everyone's thing. Who doesn't think too much? I mean, besides the doorman at Barfly."

"I mean your weakness. You overthink and then you don't act. Unless, of course, your dick is involved."

You bit your lip.

"What is it?" he said.

"We should get a bottle. You want to go get a bottle?"

He laughed. "Who are you asking?"

"I'll be back in five."

"Relax, partner," he said. "We're in this together."

*

YOU AWOKE ON THE floor in a jaundiced puddle of morning sunshine to Harrison's wheezing and a petulant knocking on the door.

"Housecleaning!" called a female voice.

Another volley of knocks. You tried to get up. The room spun; your heart hammered in your chest as though you'd passed your dreams in flight from something terrifying and your limbs felt unnaturally heavy, like the blood pumping through your veins had been transfused with viscous, bourbon ooze. A half-empty fifth of Jim Beam, parked like a road sign on the nightstand, came into focus and you dashed to the bathroom, barely making it to the toilet before releasing a stream of hot, syrupy vomit.

Another knock. "No gracias!" you yelled, mustering whatever poorly constructed high school Spanish you could. "Muchas gracias. No quiero limpiar!"

"Hey!" called the voice. "I don't speak Spanish!" Ordinarily you might have been horrified by the faux pas, but at the moment you didn't care. All that mattered was that the knocking stop and the person leave you in peace. Your heart rate slowed from a sprint to a jog. You lifted your head from the toilet bowl and bent over the sink. The water from the tap turned gradually from beige to yellow and you drank lustily, cooling your vomit-scalded esophagus. You crawled back to your spot on the floor and curled into a quivering ball of acute self-loathing. Your cell phone rattled on the table. You crawled on your hands and knees, bumping the bedside table and knocking a lamp to the floor in the process. Harrison mumbled something and turned over on his side but didn't wake. Without checking the number, you flipped open the phone.

"Hello?"

"Josh?" said an incomprehensibly youthful voice.

"Yeah?"

"It's Adrienne."

"Who?" you croaked.

"Dude. What's up with your voice? Do you have the flu or something?"

"*Adrienne?*"

"Are you sure you're all right?"

"Adrienne!" you said. "Holy... Wow! What's up? How did you..."

"I got your number from Tim. He was totally grumpy today too. What happens to you guys on Fridays? I figured you'd both be cheerful because you don't have to see any teenagers today."

"We have teenovers," you said.

"What?"

"Nothing."

"Was that a joke?"

"No. Yes."

"Jesus."

You rubbed your eyes vigorously, as though clarity of sight and thought had a direct correlation to one another. "Where've you been?"

"Play rehearsals," she said. "Every day until seven. Frank has been helping me with my geometry, which totally sucks because he doesn't know what the hell he's talking about and he just gets angry when I tell him that he's wrong."

"Play rehearsals?"

"It's nothing. These little student-written one-acts that the drama department does to kick off the school year."

"No kidding? That's rad."

"I didn't say anything because I was embarrassed. And I didn't think I'd get the part, so, better to fail quietly than be forced to endure a bunch of 'you'll get em next time, kiddo' speeches."

"That's a very Adrienne thing to say."

She laughed. You hoisted yourself into a chair and sat up straight, trying to remove the hangover from your voice. "So?"

"So I called because I'm having trouble with some aspects of this character and the director is like this totally gross guy whose sweaters reek of old man and mothballs and he always has dried spittle in the corners of his mouth, and I thought that maybe you, because I remember you said that you used to be an actor or a playwright or something, maybe you could meet with me on Friday afternoons for a few weeks at The Homework Club because I don't have rehearsal that day. Tim said it would be okay."

"He did?"

"Yep."

Warmth spread through your chest like last night's Baker's. For a moment you feared you might cry. "I'd really like that."

"Cool."

You were quiet for a few seconds until it dawned on you that she was waiting for an answer to a question. "You mean like *today* Friday?"

"Geez, that's one powerful teenover you've got there. Yes. Today."

You surveyed the wrecked motel room, trying to get your bearings. Daylight spilled through the curtains onto Harrison's sparsely bearded cheeks; cigarette butts floated in half-filled beer bottles; the gnarled and nubby blue blanket, beneath which you'd passed out, lay twisted across the middle of the floor like roadkill.

"I don't know," you said. You were visited by an image of June, leaving your apartment last night without saying a word, toting that behemoth of a duffel bag. "There's a situation I've got to take care of."

"Sounds mysterious."

You cleared your throat. "What time do I meet you there?"

"I'll be done with school at three thirty. Frank can drop me off by four."

"What time is it now?"

"Did I wake you up or something?"

"Of course not." You scanned the room for an alarm clock and realized, to your relief, that it was only ten forty-five. "Whoa. ten forty-five already. Where did my morning go?"

"Yeah, right. See you at three thirty?"

"Count on it."

You left without waking Harrison and ventured onto the street in search of your car. Your limbs felt like they were weighted down with cement blocks, and with each step, a pair of screws twisted deeper into your temples. A passing bus squealed and belched to a stop six inches from your elbow and your heart pounded so violently you feared it might crack your ribcage. The light reflecting off your car's windshield made it impossible to see the parking ticket until you were inside looking out. In addition to the hangover, you were starting the day forty-five dollars in the red.

A block from home you swerved into the 7-Eleven parking lot. Years ago this had been a grocery store, a quaint species long since extinct that had sold fresh produce and had a deli counter with a real butcher. Your dad had a tab there, an impossibly old world concept. You recalled how he used wait in the car while you ran in and grabbed a Gatorade on the way back from basketball practice. Hal the butcher would smile and wave and boast about his Los Angeles Lakers and then you'd be out the door. You got such a kick out of not paying, even if the item was being discreetly entered into a ledger. It made the store feel like an extension of your own kitchen, but with candy, sugar cereal, and soda.

The lot was empty except for a battered silver Civic hatchback taking up half of a handicapped spot and half of the neighboring space. Welded to the driver's side door was the kind of slide latch lock usually seen in bathroom stalls. *An honest person owns this vehicle*, you thought. *A person who identifies something broken and fixes it.* You wished you could approach problem solving in so straightforward a manner.

Shielding your eyes from the malevolent sunshine, you crossed the threshold into the convenience store. The electric door chime announced to the cashier—absent from his post behind the cash register—the arrival of another customer in need of a sixty-four-ounce soda, a *People* magazine, or one of yesterday's egg salad sandwiches. You cracked open a lemon-lime Gatorade and drank lustily. The chilled liquid lubricated your desiccated tongue, your acid-charred throat and induced a state of severe brain freeze. As you massaged your temples, the unmistakable sensation of being watched broke through the grimy film of your hangover. Beneath the monitor displaying the latest Lotto numbers, stood a massive man, about 6'5" with a belly the size of a cannonball hanging so precipitously over the front of his grey sweatpants that it appeared wholly possible it might break off from his torso and crack open the laminate floor. He smiled and you averted your gaze, fearful of being caught staring. You waited a beat and looked again. His eyes, now fixed on the monitor, were hidden behind black rubber sunglasses. His salt and pepper hair was matted and thick with grease, and snow-white stubble dusted his wan cheeks. He shoveled a fistful of nachos into his face and wiped the residual cheese from his fingers onto his black sweatshirt. Owing to the abuse his body had endured, it was difficult to estimate his age, but regardless of how long that body been on the planet, it could no longer be considered young. This man had been ravaged by something more aggressive than time.

You poured yourself a cup of French Roast and scrutinized the monitor. A new set of numbers tumbled across the bottom of the screen. The massive man fished into his sweatshirt pocket, took out a stub of paper, read it, and returned it to his pocket without making a sound. He stuck his finger into the mess of chili, cheese, and jalapeños, pushing the ingredients around until he uncovered a soggy chip. Bile ascended your esophagus and you quickly averted your eyes. You emptied four sugar packets into your coffee. Apropos of nothing, the massive man spoke.

"'I can resist anything but temptation.'" He lowered his sunglasses to the bridge of his nose and squinted at you. His irises were the pale blue of a scorched, late-afternoon sky. They were the lone feature, other than his voice, that possessed the slightest trace of delicacy, and yet, when fixed on you, they became the dominant feature, overhauling your initial impression. "Oscar Wilde." He winked. "Forgive my being so bold as to presume that you, like I, might have firsthand knowledge of the sentiment's truth."

You broke from his gaze and busied your hands with the task of peeling back the little foil lids on the single-servings of Half and Half. "Your powers of perception are prodigious."

"It does not take great acuity to recognize one's own."

You nodded but kept your focus on your task; you stirred your coffee, blew on it, and took a tentative sip.

He sighed. "Perhaps a different career path would have bolstered my self-discipline."

"I'm a teacher," you said suddenly, surprising yourself.

He smiled. "Aha. And I a student."

"I work with teenagers. They're a pain in the ass but when you get through to them, you know, the ones that can still be gotten through to..."

"Yours is a noble profession. You are an asset to both your students and your community."

You fitted a lid to your steaming coffee. Having no idea where you were going with this, you could do nothing but blush and change the subject. "Where's the cashier?"

The man returned his gaze to the monitor. "Habib!" he yelled. No one responded. "A teacher wishes to make a purchase!"

You immediately recognized the handsome, doe-eyed Indian man with a neatly trimmed mustache who emerged from a door labeled *Employees Only*. He'd rung you up on many occasions but you'd never spoken to one another.

"So sorry," he said. "I am understaffed today and I was... I had to..."

"Habib is as fine a man as you will find in this country today—a recently naturalized citizen with the kind of work ethic rarely observed in our homegrown residents."

Habib shook his head and scanned your coffee cup and half-empty Gatorade. "Thank you, sir. So sorry to keep you waiting."

"It's fine," you said. "Habib?"

"Yes. Thank you," he said, turning his back on you and tearing open a giant stack of shrink-wrapped *Playboy*s.

You stopped on your way out the door. "My name's Josh, by the way."

Habib's head swiveled.

"I'm sorry?"

"I'm Josh. I live around the corner."

Both men stared at you but neither spoke. Your cheeks burned red.

"A local of our fair province," said the massive man.

You smiled. "Actually, I grew up nearby but I hadn't lived in the Valley for years until I moved back a few months ago."

"The prodigal son," he said with a satisfied grin. "My name is Ozzie. Some call me Wizard."

"No shit!" you said. He furrowed his brow. "My buddies, Bill and Amare...they're great admirers of yours."

The Wizard nodded knowingly, as if he had intuited this precise connection the moment you walked in and was now savoring his clairvoyance like a mouthful of chile cheese sauce. He piloted another chip towards his cavernous mouth and sighed as he chewed. "Tell me, Josh. Have you read Yeats?"

"Not since high school."

"Care to test that memory?"

You pinched the bridge of your nose. "I had a pretty rough night." The Wizard kept right on chewing, as thought you hadn't said a word.

"Okay," you said. "Try me."

He smiled and straightened to his full height. "'The blood-dimmed tide is loosed,'" he shoveled another chile-cheese-soaked chip into his mouth and spoke as he chewed. "And everywhere the ceremony of innocence is drowned." He tilted his head, swallowed his food, lifted his eyebrows.

"No, I recognize it." Your heart sank. It was suddenly very important that you impress this man.

"The best lack all conviction," he said.

"Shit," you said. "Shit, shit."

"While the worst…"

"Something," you said, snapping your fingers. "Something, about intensity."

The Wizard raised his chin, teetering on the precipice of praise.

"They're full of it!" you said. "Are *full* of passionate intensity."

"Very good, young man!" he bellowed. With his free hand, he patted his belly. "The question that remains to be seen, Joshua, is 'what rough beast, its hour come round at last, slouches towards Bethlehem to be born?'"

"Seems to me we've got no shortage of rough beasts these days."

He laughed and scratched his white whiskers. "Tell those radiant young lads that The Wizard sends his greetings."

*

THE APARTMENT WAS SUNNY and surprisingly well ventilated; the boys, seated respectively at the computer and the dining table, appeared fresh and well groomed. They turned blank, inscrutable faces in your direction.

"What?"

"Where've you been?" said Amare.

"Aw," you said. "You guys worried about me?" You tossed your keys on the table and sat beside Bill, his nearly completed Whole Foods application between his elbows. "Well look at you. Way to go, man."

"Where's your girl?" said Amare.

"Please don't call her that."

"She never came home either," said Bill. "She left a message, saying she was out and that she'd try your cell. That was the last we heard from her."

You checked your phone. No missed calls. "I was so hammered last night," you said, sipping your coffee and staring out the window at the neighboring apartment building, its cracked stucco walls and opaque windows caked with grime. You hadn't thought of it as dumpy until now. At night, its flickering blue lights and electrical buzz created the impression of animation, but daylight revealed the totality of its decrepitude.

"I guess I remember talking to her," you said, knowing full well that such a conversation never took place.

"Where is she?" said Bill.

"Her girlfriend's, I think," you said, embellishing the lie. "I'll track her down after work."

"I thought you didn't have to go in on Fridays," said Bill. "Was hoping you could drive me over to Whole Foods to drop this thing off."

"New gig, but no worries. I can drop it off on my way."

"Don't you think I should do it in person?"

"I don't think it matters. I'll tell what's her name…"

"Sadie."

"Right. I'll tell her how excited you are and whatnot."

You sat on the couch and stared at the muted TV, last night's sports highlights flickering frivolously before your eyes, a montage of fragments to be consumed and immediately forgotten.

"Oh!" you said brightly. "I finally met the famous Wizard over at 7-Eleven. What a character."

Amare popped up from his seat at the computer. "He still there?"

"Didn't look like he was going anywhere."

Amare crammed his bare feet into his shoes and made for the door.

"What's so urgent?" you said.

"Gotta see if my numbers came up."

"Say it ain't so," said Bill.

"Beats working at a grocery store."

"That's right," Bill mumbled as Amare opened the front door. "The Wizard's got it all figured out."

You patted Bill on the shoulder, pointed at the application. "You want me to take that?"

Bill signed his name to it and pushed it in front of you where it absorbed a couple drops of spilt coffee.

"Shit," he said, dabbing the spots with the sleeve of his shirt.

"Don't worry about it," you said. "Besides, I got it on good authority that the world is coming to an end."

"The sooner the better."

You laughed; Bill stared morosely at the television. "Hey," you said. "Bill."

"I shouldn't watch these highlights anymore," he said. On the screen, images of yesterday's Red Sox game played out mutely.

"I feel like this year is going to be the ultimate cocktease. If we just had a closer, we could win this whole goddamned thing!"

"I hear you." You reclined and the weary rattan back of your dining room chair moaned. You patted Bill's knee and folded your hands on your stomach.

Bill said, "If the Yankees beat us again this year, I'm gonna break into Fenway and set myself on fire in left field. Right where Yaz's legs buckled when Bucky Dent hit the home run in seventy-eight."

You nodded approvingly. "Sounds like a plan."

"You want to join me? Dual self-immolations to protest years of incompetent ownership."

"Justice for the fans!" you said.

Bill turned the television off and sighed. He leaned forward, rested his elbows on his knees. "It must be nice working with kids sometimes. I could never do it but I get why you do."

"This girl I'm working with today, she's kind of my favorite person. She's this really bright, irreverent goth-chick with green hair and black eye shadow. You know, one of those kids that sees through the bullshit and is righteously pissed off, but beneath all that is a sweet and vulnerable girl who just wants to be liked."

"What's she need tutoring for?"

"She doesn't need tutoring." You went to the kitchen and got some Advil from the cabinet. "Her parents basically send her there to be supervised."

"Rich assholes."

You nodded. "I'm glad she's there though. She's always worried about something, always stressed. She doesn't recognize how capable she is. But I feel like she listens to me, like, when I point out that it takes real strength to question what her school and her parents tell her she's supposed to want, it resonates."

Bill rubbed his head. "My parents want me to come home. They think I'm wasting my time."

"They said that?"

"They're about as subtle as a sledgehammer."

You glanced at the clock. If you were going to get to Whole Foods on the way to work, it was time to get moving.

"Do *you* think you're wasting your time?" you said.

"What else is time good for?" He sat up and scanned the room, his eyes coming to rest on the table. "Is it cool if I bum one of your cigarettes?"

"Go for it."

He shook one free and stuck it between his lips.

"I don't know how you do that," you said.

"What?"

"Smoke occasionally. I'm envious I guess."

"Being an addict takes energy." You laughed as he crossed the room and went out onto the balcony.

"You're too tired to get addicted to smoking?"

He stood in the doorframe, lamely holding the cigarette outside. Smoke streamed, unabated, into the living room. "No idea when June's coming home?"

"None. Why?"

He shrugged. "I don't know. She's good to talk to. She's got so many crises. In a way her life is even duller than mine, but she always manages to have this air of urgency about her."

A throb passed through your temples and you winced.

"Is that a fucked up thing to say?"

"No." You rubbed your head with your thumbs.

He took a drag of the cigarette, turned his head and attempted to blow the smoke outside but a breeze carried it right back through the doorway. "Tell Sadie that I hope she sees it in her heart to rescue me from a life of sloth and mooching."

You laughed. "You should put that on your resume under current occupation."

Bill stared at his cigarette. "I don't want any more of this."

"You had like two drags."

He shrugged. "You finish it." He rubbed off the cherry and it dropped to the balcony floor where he crushed it beneath his shoe. Then he crossed the room, holding out the half-smoked cigarette, and dropped it in your open palm. The two of you stared.

*

A LINE TEN CARS deep idled in the far right lane of Coldwater Canyon, waiting to gain entry to the Whole Foods parking lot. Typical Angelinos, many of them transplants from metropolitan areas where parking is scarce, refused to park more than a block from their destination. Not shelling out for the valet at a restaurant was a sign of abject poverty tantamount to taking the bus. You drove past the line, turned onto a familiar residential street and parked outside the house at which June had been crashing when you first started dating. Staring at the selfsame magnolia tree beneath which you'd parked every night for the first six months of your relationship, your chest swelled with nostalgia. You thought of those stories of pregnant women whose hormones cause them to weep at maudlin tire commercials. How completely fucked you were to desire a return to something so broken, a delirium that had propelled you down a landslide of poor decisions, lost opportunities, and broken promises. Your infatuation had been one big humiliation, a blind spot that had obfuscated what everyone else saw coming a mile away.

In the middle of June's former neighbor's yard, a defiant American flag flapped in the faces of all the secular progressives who'd gobbled up the properties surrounding the neighborhood Fox News viewer, a curmudgeon of the first order who used to yell at the two of you for laughing in the backyard past 10:00 p.m. You recalled the first time you'd really minded that flag, the first time it filled you with a sense of impending doom.

"I want to be with you at the end of the world," June had said when the towers came tumbling down. She put her head on your shoulder as your restless feet rocked the patio swing back and forth, back and forth. "We can tell each other anything, whatever we're feeling, and know that no matter what, we'll be safe because we won't be alone." You were speechless. All day long you'd been wolfing down coffee, cigarettes, and television news, dreading the moment when you would have to stop consuming and close your eyes. Then there was June, taking your hand, trying to coax out feelings that you ordinarily dissembled beneath a veneer of equanimity and Xanax.

You'd gone back inside, turned off the television and returned to her room—an unmade bed of twisted sheets already imbued with the memory of the first frightening phone call from your father—and made love like the problems of the world were nothing but a storm cloud blown back out to sea.

"I want to see my mom," she said, as you lay beneath the ceiling fan, panting and sweating in one another's arms. "Will you go with me? It would make her happy to see you with me."

"She hardly knows me."

"I think she thinks that as long as I'm with you, she can die in peace."

You sat up, frowning. You had an inkling of what you were supposed to say here, but you couldn't bring yourself to form the words. Besides, it had been a long morning. Perhaps staring at footage of bodies dropping like tears from the faces of crumbling skyscrapers was making her mom's demise feel more imminent.

She stared at the ceiling, her tangled hair fanned out across the pillow; beads of perspiration glistened on her forehead. Cinematically, she turned her gaze to the open window and spoke the words, "My mom's really sick." You braced for tears but she didn't cry; judging by the tone of her voice, you guessed that it would be a long time before she would.

June proceeded to reveal the truth about her mom's cancer and her resistance to treatment, a resistance that sounded more like a resignation to die than the fear of fighting. Until that day, June hadn't wanted to talk about her mom, and you hadn't encouraged her to go opening fresh wounds. Now you needed more information. Because it hadn't occurred to you that there might be people hoping that June would end up with you. Your desire for a lasting commitment was like the cure for cancer—yet to be discovered. June's mother's hope—that you might be the one whom, in the event of her death, looked after her picky little girl—was a powerful revelation.

That afternoon the two of you walked, down this street and others just like it—residential and tree-lined. "All these pretty green lawns," she said.

She walked like she didn't want to get anywhere, as if the faster she moved, the closer she would draw to a future she feared she couldn't avoid, no matter her footwork, her partner, her pills, her plans. A pick-up truck with oversized tires drove by, blasting some country-western dreck; an American flag, thrust out the open window by a proud, pale, patriotic arm, flapped in the wind.

"What the fuck," she said.

"That's only gonna get worse."

"It's true," she said.

"First it'll be flags and anthems, then it'll be demonizing Muslims. War with some impoverished Middle Eastern country will be an easy sell. The Democrats will fall in line because they'll be afraid to look like pussies with our dimwitted cowboy of a president swinging his dick around and, meanwhile, there'll be no self-reflection, no accountability, no rethinking of..."

She took your hand. "Josh."

You stopped.

She kissed you, stroked your cheek. "I love you," she said. Then she wrapped her arms around your waist and kissed you some more. A neighbor walked by, dragged by a large, panting dog, but June didn't seem to notice. Ordinarily, she was uncomfortable with public displays of affection; you'd learned to resist the urge to touch without first gauging her mood. Not that this bothered you; in fact, it made physical contact that much more meaningful. Because it wasn't habit, you felt like each touch was deliberate, compelled by a fresh feeling. For all her faults, June's love was never stale. Sometimes it simply wasn't. But this made it all the more thrilling when it was. And on that particular day, with her mother dying and New York City's iconic skyline crumbling, entropy amplified your love. You were one another's solace.

You returned from your reverie, gripping your phone. You tried to summon the strength to push these memories down into some dark, inaccessible place, but in your brief life, there'd only been one dying mother whose frail hand you'd held amongst the cloying stink of get-well bouquets and made a promise.

You dialed. Her phone rang twice and stopped. You heard voices, the clatter of silverware and porcelain, the faint peal of a siren.

"Hello?" you said.

"I didn't know if I was going to hear from you." Her voice was flat, detached. You drew air into your lungs as though you were preparing to retrieve rings from the deep end of the pool. You exhaled. "Aren't you going to ask where I am?"

"Where are you?"

"What difference does that make?"

"Where did you go last night?"

"I need a ride home."

"Home, as in my apartment?"

"Is it your mission in life to make me feel shitty?"

You absorbed the body blow and pressed forward. "I've gotta work. Tell me where you are and I'll pick you up in a couple hours."

June was quiet. The siren wailed louder and louder.

"Or you could take the bus."

"I'll call someone else."

"That'd probably be better...for you I mean."

"Right."

The connection severed. The American flag hung limply in the hot still air, its colors bleaching in the implacable sunshine.

*

WHOLE FOODS GREETED YOU with a thick wall of conditioned air. Sadie rang up items at the far register. For a few seconds you watched her deftly scoop, scan, tap the register keys, and chat with a customer. It was easy to tell that she was good at her job. You guessed she'd had a lot of practice. As far as you knew, she'd worked there since high school. You wondered what dreams she'd put on hold, whether she'd tried another career and failed, returning to this place with her tail between her legs. Whatever her story was, her posture, the way she rooted her feet so firmly in the ground and held her chin high, projected confidence unconstrained by regret.

You ventured into the aisles in search of peanut butter, but the only kind that you could find was the hippie shit with the puddle of oil on top that you had to stir every time you wanted to make a sandwich—the kind of product that no self-respecting 7-Eleven owner would dare peddle. You read the brief list of ingredients on half a dozen different brands. None of the Whole Foods peanut butters seemed to contain sugar. Some of them didn't even have salt. Other than some poor soul with congestive heart failure and a low-sodium-or-death diet, you couldn't imagine who would buy this stuff. Finally, you discovered a brand containing something called *evaporated cane juice*. Close enough, you thought.

You filed into Sadie's queue, peanut butter in tow; she caught sight of you out of the corner her eye and winked, as if she'd either already known you were in the store or had been anticipating your return. The old man in front of you, dandruff dusting the shoulders of his navy blue cardigan, scratched his closely cropped white hair and pointed at the register display.

"What's that?" he said.

"Your total, sir," said Sadie. "Sixty-four dollars and fourteen cents."

"I only bought food for tonight," he said. "I'm having my daughter and my grandson over for dinner. He's four years old, eats like a squirrel. You think I need to spend sixty-four dollars to feed my daughter and a squirrel?"

Sadie smiled at you. Not nervously, like you would have expected, but inclusively, as if the truth of her job didn't embarrass her in the least.

"Would you like me to ring up the items again, sir? Maybe I made a mistake."

"Ring 'em again." The old man turned to you. "Gotta keep an eye on 'em and make sure they don't scan anything twice. These people make mistakes all the time."

You shrugged. "She looks trustworthy to me."

Sadie debagged and rescanned. Boneless chicken breasts, teriyaki sauce, green beans, a few lemons, a bottle of wine, a bottle of cranberry juice, and some chocolate chocolate chip ice cream. "I'm sorry, sir, but it's still sixty-four-fourteen. Would you maybe like to put something back?"

His fingers trembling, the man struggled to remove his credit card from his wallet before grudgingly handing it over. "Charge it," he said. "Thieves is what you all are. I could have taken them out for steak dinners."

"At Sizzler maybe," you said.

"Excuse me?"

"Nothing," you said.

Sadie stifled a laugh. The man's head whipped around and she coughed to mask her smile. He glared at her and then you, before pushing his cart of groceries through the sliding doors.

"I'm an asshole," you said.

"Don't sweat it. He's a regular. He knows the prices. I think that half the time he just comes in here for an outlet."

"Here." You handed over the application. "I told Bill I'd give this to you on my way to work. He doesn't have a car yet."

"Cool." She gave the application a cursory glance and placed it next to the register. "I like Bill. He's funny."

"Bill's hilarious. And a hard worker to boot."

"He told me that I reminded him of a cousin he had a giant crush on when he was a boy."

You laughed. "Really?"

"Yep," she said, grinning. She scanned your peanut butter. "Ooh. I love this stuff, but I get the crunchy kind. So good."

"I have to admit, ordinarily I'm a Skippy man."

"Oh no, no, no," she said, shaking her head side to side and clicking her tongue. "We must reform you, Joshua. Once you develop a palate for the natural stuff, you'll never go back to that processed crap, no matter how sweet your tooth."

You stroked your cheek and nodded, as though she'd addressed a character flaw of serious consequence.

"Six-fifty-two," she said.

Your eyes widened but you caught yourself in time to suppress any other physical indicators of outrage and handed her a ten.

Sadie took your money and opened the cash drawer. As she withdrew three ones she smiled coyly and said, "The same principle applies to women you know." Then she laughed, whether in response to your startled expression or her own brazenness you couldn't tell. You blushed intensely. Sadie was flirting with you. It dawned on you that she wasn't embarrassed by the sex you'd had years ago; she appeared to be interested in who you were now, not who you had or hadn't been then.

"Avoid the processed ones?" you said.

"At all costs." She broke the seal on a roll of quarters and spilled some on the floor. "Oh Sadie," she scolded, bending over and surfaced like a diver coming up for air. The squint of her eyes issued a gentle challenge and quickened your pulse. You stared at them for a beat too long without saying anything; a self-satisfied smile spread across her face and she handed you your change. The middle-aged woman behind you, who'd unloaded enough groceries from her cart to feed a junior varsity basketball team, cleared her throat.

"Afternoon, miss," Sadie said, grabbing a pair of romaine lettuce heads and entering their code from memory. "You having a nice day?"

"Yeah, yeah," said the woman.

You shoved your change into your pocket and drifted away like a leaf carried on the surface of a stream.

"See you soon, Josh?" called Sadie, an unmistakable question mark affixed to your name.

You stopped, carts and their impatient captains piling up behind you. "Yeah," you said. "Definitely."

In a daze, you stepped in front of a hulking Land Rover and it came to a lurching halt. The incredulous driver, an orange-skinned woman with platinum blond hair, raised her hands in the universal what-the-fuck gesture of exasperation. You smiled and waved. "Hey," you said, to which she scowled. You walked the one residential block to your car, thinking about Sadie. About how she didn't so neatly fit into any of the categories you'd identified for people your age: those who put their careers first, those who put humanity first, those who put art first, and those without agency, who put nothing first unless it was put there by someone else. Sadie was an outlier. You wanted to know more—

what motivated her, what scared her, where she wanted to go, whether she still bit the tip of her thumb during sex.

Leaves blew down June's old street. On the sidewalk, a black and white spotted cat lounged in a splash of sunshine. You approached it steadily, its eyes gray and lazy, the sunshine having lulled it into languorous inertia. You took a knee and it rolled onto its side, allowing you to stroke its soft belly fur. You hoped you'd never be too preoccupied to see the sunshine splashes in the landscape of each waking day. Suddenly, without warning, the cat struck out with a precise paw. You yanked your hand back, but a jagged claw caught your flesh, leaving behind angry pink slash. Droplets of blood quickly appeared. You sucked on the wound and spit, as the still supine cat watched, its paw poised for another strike should you have the gall to pet it again.

"I thought we were friends," you said.

The cat yawned and looked away.

You drove to The Homework Club, thinking of a night about a year before in a sleazy nightclub with Harrison—women and their sweat-glistened flesh; drunken men drooling like overheated boys, facing an array of ice cream flavors without the protective pane of glass. The room was sticky and humid—a viscous secretion on the tip of Hollywood's erect cock. You'd told Harrison that you didn't know what you were doing there. When he said that you were still a man and a man was allowed to look, you just laughed, confessed that looking did nothing for you. These women had nothing on your girl.

"You're hopeless," he said.

You agreed, happily, so privileged to be beyond the reach of sultry strangers, to have all your desire funneled towards a single living and breathing person whom you could cradle in your arms.

You drove home that night, eager to demonstrate your passion, but June was nowhere to be found. Ever since Harrison had witnessed her temper, she'd thrown fits when the two of you hung out, convinced that the majority of your time together was spent plotting ways to leave her. At four in the morning, she staggered inside dead drunk, stripped and collapsed into bed. Your heart pounded in your chest while you waited for her to say something. You got out of bed, put on your robe and ventured downstairs for a smoke, took a slug of whiskey for good measure. By the time you returned to bed, you'd calmed down. Hurt people hurt people. June couldn't be blamed for fearing you'd desert her like everyone else.

You nestled up beside her, skin against skin, and put your arm around her stomach. Her head moved ever so slightly and her hand found your wrist. "You reek," she said and threw your arm off of her.

You moved to the other side of the bed and watched her naked back rise and fall in feigned sleep. Her nudity mocked you. Dangled tantalizingly close, she dared you to take her by force, to make yourself the villain, to demonstrate that you were as wretched and vulgar as the rest of them. It made you so deeply sad, for you and for her, that she wouldn't let you share what was in your heart.

*

IN THE MEAGER SHADE provided by the Homework Club awning, Adrienne, the other woman in your life, leisurely read a paperback. You watched from your car as she lifted her head and stared out into space from behind a pair of pink-rimmed Ray-Bans, contemplating whatever nugget of wisdom she'd just absorbed. Apparently she hadn't seen you pull up to the curb. You had dichotomous urges to either jump out of the car and give her a hug, or drive to the coast, sit on an isolated beach and let the waves usher you into the type of trance that your worries could not infiltrate. Your head ached. It was going to take a good long nap or a gallon of coffee to get you through the day.

Still tingling your extremities was the residue of Sadie's flirtations. But even if you were interested, what could you do? Your ex-ish girlfriend was sleeping in your bed and there was no good explanation for it. In your gut, helping June made sense, but your gut had a lousy fucking memory.

You got out of the car and threw your arms wide. "All the world's a stage!" you bellowed over the street noise. "And all the Joshes and Adriennes merely players."

She peered over the top of her sunglasses, looking at you as though you were a circus clown or some other childhood relic long since outgrown.

You unlocked the door to the Homework Club and held it open. "'Once more unto the breach, dear friends.'"

"I can't believe I asked for this."

"Relax. That's the extent of my Shakespeare."

"That's it? I thought you were an actor."

"I was." The room was stuffy. You switched on the air conditioning and began taking the chairs down from the table nearest the window. "An aspiring film actor. I did a lot of theater in college but Hollywood has no patience for substance."

"That sounds like a cop out."

"It's the truth." You lowered yourself into a chair and rubbed the bridge of your nose. "I took some classes after I came home, wanted to stay sharp. My teacher assigned me a scintillating scene study of *Feeling Minnesota* before I gave it all up to write my own crappy screenplays and tutor the likes of you."

"*Feeling Minnesota*? That's a movie?"

"What they call in the industry a 'rom com', featuring the comedic stylings of Keanu Reeves and Cameron Diaz."

"Jesus Christ. That sounds torturous."

"No. Torture was having to watch a duo in my class workshop a series of Miller Light commercials."

"Now you are joking."

"I wouldn't do that to you, Adrienne. I have too much respect for you. Best that you know the ugly truth about this profession from the start. It's positively soul-crushing to discover such things after years of harboring grand illusions about meaning and truth."

"That's not gonna happen to me," she said. "If I decide to be an actor, I'm going to be a stage actor. I don't care about money and fame."

You bit your lip. "Fair enough."

Her tone informed you that you'd arrived at that moment when, as a teacher, you needed to jettison the sarcasm and let the obvious contradictions in her statement slide. Ushered around in a luxury SUV by a man in a tuxedo, attending a private school with an annual tuition of at least thirty thousand dollars, the beneficiary of daily tutoring for the better part of high school, and the soon-to-be applicant at a number of liberal arts colleges that would cost an easy quarter million, Adrienne managed to say that she didn't care about money with a straight face. Maybe it was true. Maybe she would have given it all up to go to public school, live in a modest Valley apartment, and eat dinner with her parents every night. Only time would tell.

But eschewing capitalism after twenty-two some-odd years of suckling at its teat was easier said than done.

The two of you rehearsed a scene that had been giving her a lot of trouble, a difficult scene for a tenth grader because of the homoerotic subtext. The scene, between two housewives, purported to be about gardening techniques. Adrienne didn't get it. She thought it was a useless piece of dialogue and could not for the life of her decipher any source of tension. You could see why the director had cast her in the part; the problem was that she couldn't. She resorted to trying to find drama in the text and performed the lines as though the meaning was on the surface.

"You need to write another set of dialogue," you said.

"What do you mean?"

You tapped the script. "An unspoken line of dialogue for each spoken one. These words have a literal meaning, but what else is your character trying to express?"

She frowned. "I don't know."

"We, people, all of us, we're always after something, right? Otherwise, what use would we have for language?"

"Language was created so we could exchange ideas."

"Ideas that would help us get our greedy hands on what we wanted but didn't have. Whether that's admiration, food, power, sex, or inner peace, desire is at the root of all communication."

Adrienne blushed.

"I'm sorry," you said. "I didn't mean to embarrass you."

"You think this scene is about sex?"

You shrugged. "Maybe. At least partially."

Her eyes opened wide. She looked accusingly at the script and then back at you. "My character is like, in love with her friend. That's it, right?"

"Yes."

"But they're both married."

"True."

"To men."

You bit your tongue. She inhaled loudly through her flared nostrils, brought the script within a few inches of her face and squinted, as though the words, if viewed through a magnifying lens, might reveal their true intent.

You leaned back in your chair. "You could make it be about something else if you wanted to—just as long as this scene isn't a conversation about the virtues of tomatoes over cucumbers. You don't want to subject your audience to that."

"Dammit!" she said and slammed her elbows into the table before dropping her head into her hands. "I'm so stupid!"

"C'mon now. None of that."

"My stupid drama teacher thinks I'm a lesbian just because I like poetry and I don't dress like a slut."

You patted her back. "Maybe your drama teacher just thinks that it's adult subject matter and that you can handle it."

"He thinks I'm a lesbian!"

You searched the room for a conversation piece that would allow you to gracefully change the subject. Out the window, you spied the neighboring falafel place. "You want to go next door. Get a soda?"

"Everybody thinks it!" she said, folding her arms on the table in front of her, burying her face in them and convulsing with a series of jagged sobs.

"Adrienne," you said, wanting desperately to put an arm around her. But The Homework Club was empty, and you had strict rules about physical contact with students you were alone with.

She raised her face from the table, wiped her eyes with the sleeve of her red and black checkered shirt. "I'm not a lesbian."

"Okay," you said, folding your hands in your lap and trying, with your tone and your eyes, to convey as much compassion as humanly possible. "I believe you. But if you were, it wouldn't matter."

"Would you please listen to me? I'm in love with someone! And he's not a girl. He's older than me and he's sensitive and smart and beautiful."

The emptiness inside the Homework Club, the absence of teenagers and bosses and tutors, expanded around you like the silence that follows an ill-timed joke. Your stomach dropped as Adrienne's eyes beseeched you to believe.

"Adrienne."

"His name is Corey. He's the lead in the play and he plays the guitar and sings and he probably thinks I'm a lesbian too!"

You closed your eyes and thanked whatever there was to thank that you weren't the smart, sensitive, older guy.

"Josh?"

"Seriously," you said. "Soda time." You stood up and put on your baseball cap. "You gonna join me?"

"Soda has corn syrup."

"Adrienne."

"Corn syrup causes cirrhosis."

You frowned. "Seriously?"

"Seriously. It can't be metabolized. Your liver needs to filter it out of your body."

"One soda?"

She huffed. "Fine."

You opened the door to Pita Time! and the smell of the shawarma you'd ingested daily for months hit you like a left hook. Your stomach, like Amare subjected to mainstream media or Bill subjected to the Red Sox bullpen, struggled to maintain its composure. You ordered a ginger ale and bought Adrienne a Dr. Pepper. The two of you sat at the counter, quietly sipping as the saccharine liquid lacquered your respective worries and poisoned your essential organs.

"I need a vacation," she said.

"I hear you."

"Really. If it weren't for the play, I think I'd just stop turning in homework until my school threatened to expel me and my parents sent me away to some kind of boarding school."

You didn't know how to respond. As an employee of her parents, your duty here was clearly to encourage her to stay the course. But you didn't even know her parents, they never took the time to come down and talk about their daughter, and if you were being honest, her idea didn't sound so misguided. If anyone needed to get away from home, it was Adrienne. As small of a window as two-and-a-half years might sound to an adult, it's a lifetime to a fifteen year old. Who knew how much counseling she'd have to undergo to undo two-and-a-half years of damage inflicted by callous peers?

"I think that you should keep working hard. Giving up is a tough habit to break."

Adrienne pondered this for a minute, chewing on her soda straw. "It smells like cat vomit in here," she said.

You laughed. "You want to go for a walk?"

"What, and suck car exhaust? No thanks. Let's just go back and work on the scene. You can teach me all about the virtues of boobs…I mean tomatoes."

"Adrienne!" You widened your eyes in faux shock.

She giggled, covering her mouth with her hand.

"How much time do we have?" she said. "Could you stay an extra thirty minutes? I have some geometry proofs that I have no idea how to do."

"Nothing would bring me greater pleasure."

"Well that's the saddest thing I've heard all day."

"Hey!" you said, putting your hand on her shoulder. "We're pals, aren't we? I missed you these last couple of weeks."

She grinned and slurped her soda.

*

THE DINER WHERE YOU retrieved June was little more than a mile from home, but upon glimpsing that onerous bag, you understood why she'd waited for a ride. Either she'd intended to disappear, or she'd wanted the bulk of her bag to convey the intention. She hoisted it into car and sank wordlessly into the passenger seat, refusing to make eye contact.

"You want to talk about it?"

"Talk about what? How I've been sitting at that diner for hours, waiting for you to pick me up?"

You rolled down your window, took a deep breath and tuned the radio to a jazz station playing early-sixties Coltrane. As you drove, she picked and bit the jagged edges of her fingernails and repeatedly cleared her throat, an old tic that made it impossible for you to be spared a single moment of her discontent. A couple blocks from the apartment, you pulled the car off the road alongside the park.

"Let's go for a walk," you said.

"Ugh."

"We can't just go on acting like nothing's changed."

She spun her head toward you, fixed you with her coal black stare. "Nothing has changed. Except that you went out last night with Harrison to talk shit about me and avoid my phone calls."

"Phone calls?"

"I could tell that you were directing me right to voice mail."

"That's not even remotely true." You dug into your pocket for your phone. "Look!" You scrolled through the index of missed and received calls. "There's not a single missed call from you here."

"Aren't you even going to ask me where I went last night?" She faced you and raised her eyebrows.

You looked out the window and took a very deep breath. "It doesn't matter, June. We're not... This is not..."

"He said he was doing anger management classes; he begged me to stay."

You gripped the steering wheel. "Please don't do this."

She laughed. "You're pathetic." Then she got out of the car, walked to a bench about ten yards away and sat down.

You opened your door and stood, one leg still inside the car. Traffic sailed by, lashing your back with gusts of warm, dusty air. "June," you said. She lit a cigarette and showed no sign of having heard you. "June!" A middle-aged woman in a red tracksuit squinted at you as she power-walked the dirt path. It took all your strength not to tell her to fuck off. You pulled her bag out of the back seat, marched over to the bench and dumped it at her feet.

"I'm done."

She glanced down, snickered and stared off into the foliage.

"You think this is funny?"

"I think it's fucking hilarious."

You pointed your finger at her. "You're not coming back to my place until you stop fucking lying. You insist on creating these alternate realities in which I'm the bad guy, I'm responsible for your fucked-up life. It's bullshit! What have I done wrong, June? What have I done besides give you food and shelter and try be a good friend?"

"A good friend who fucks me and then threatens to throw me out."

You clutched your stomach. June had knocked the wind out of you many times, but this went deeper. "I never fucking want to see you again!" you screamed, trying to smother the pain in your gut with volume. "Do you hear me? I'm fucking done with this!" June didn't so much as flinch. As if swallowed by the breeze, your words elicited no reaction. She just sat there, spine steeled, ears plugged with stony recalcitrance. Her only response to your rage—a slight tremor in the hand that brought the cigarette to her lips. No matter the context, June's pride, like a giant redwood, was a humbling thing to behold.

"I'm out of here," you said, a cold, firm cruelty supplanting your sloppy fury. You pointed at her bag. "Get one of your other boyfriends to lug your shit around, you ungrateful fucking whore."

You marched away, drove off without looking back. You accelerated past your street, swerved onto the freeway and headed west at ninety miles an hour. You tore through Valley Village, Sherman Oaks, Van Nuys. When you reached the 405 interchange, traffic slowed you to a crawl; you yelled and pummeled your car's roof with your fist. You exited the freeway and parked on a shady side street. Giant palm fronds bent and swayed with the wind, pointing long accusatory fingers.

Like any powerful emotion, while inside it, your fury felt greater than any emotion that had ever come before it. However, once outside its immediacy, it became more recognizable, identical, in fact, to the first time she had broken you—back when she wasn't totally reliant on others, before she'd blown through all her savings and Toyota of North Hollywood repossessed her car. You couldn't remember why she'd stormed out of your apartment that night, but you remembered what she'd said before she left. She was going back to her ex. If you didn't try to stop her, you'd never see her again. In that moment, you knew precisely what you should do: lock the door, reinforce it with an armful of two-by-fours *Night of the Living Dead*–style, and refuse her re-entry. But even back then, still so close to the beginning, you were too hooked to let go.

Her car door had slammed, the engine turned over, tires shrieked against the asphalt like an eagle. You grabbed your keys and sprinted outside. Your iron expression, captured by the rear view mirror as you started your car, stayed with you, as did the eerie out-of-bodiness that followed—you, watching yourself, like a character in a movie, chase her down, swerve in front of her car so that she came within a few inches of colliding with your passenger door. She reversed and began to turn, but you quickly reversed as well, blocking her escape. You yelled like a madman until June began to laugh. You lost control, yelled louder, and said vicious things until, to your horror, her laughter turned to tears. Her crying stopped you cold. Your rage vanished and what remained of you was eerily insubstantial—a shucked cornhusk left on the ground to scatter in the breeze.

"Please," you said. "Please don't go." And of course she didn't. Instead she returned to your apartment with an intimate knowledge of the contours of your dependency, while you trailed behind with the acute sense of mortality that tickles the gut after a near-death experience, your weakest moment etched indelibly into your memory, a new label to fit into your mercurial self-image—coward.

*

AS YOU PULLED UP to your apartment building, you didn't recognize the man yelling into the intercom outside the glass double doors that led to the lobby. An ephemeral thought— *been there, pal*—flitted through your brain before you opened the automatic gate leading to the covered parking lot and forgot about him entirely. You studied your reflection in the rear-view mirror and took some deep breaths. Where did the person you were with Adrienne go when you were with June? That person was an adult, replete with principles and integrity. He didn't scream, slouch, sigh, or stare into space. Maybe he was just an actor, imitating the patience, generosity, and confidence that looked so good on others.

Demoralized and deflated, you walked toward the door that led to the lobby. As you gripped the knob, the unmistakable sounds of a scuffle reached your ears: shouting cut off in mid-sentence, rubber soles squeaking on the floor like high tops in a basketball gymnasium, grunts and thuds. You swung open the door and saw a bald scalp, beet red and bleeding, in a headlock administered by the thick, tan, veiny arms of the man who had been yelling into the intercom. You froze. The tan man looked up. You'd never been introduced, but recognition was instantaneous. His black eyes narrowed and he loosened his grip on his victim, who coughed and gasped a throaty, "Fucking let go of me!" and then Reno, June's abusive ex-boyfriend, sent

Bill's oxygen-starved body sailing across the lobby so that his face collided with the bronze mailbox plates with a dull thunk and Bill collapsed like all the artistic integrity in Hollywood. Reno stared at him, crumpled there on the floor, and you didn't hesitate. You charged, threw all your weight behind your right shoulder and landed it squarely in the middle of his chest. The air evacuated his lungs and he wheezed like an old smoker as pain rocketed down your arm, all the way to your fingertips, and together you toppled to the floor where the back of his head thwacked the linoleum. You scrambled to your feet, your right arm dangling uselessly at your side, ready to kick him if you needed to, but Reno just groaned, long and low, his eyes closed, and held his head in his hands. You moved quickly to Bill, blood trickling from the cut on his scalp and his right eye slammed shut beneath a rapidly distending mouse.

"Bill!" His left eyelid fluttered. "Bill, get up!" You managed to pull him up into a seated position.

"Owwww!" Reno moaned.

Bill opened his good eye and glanced over at Reno. "Did I do that?" he slurred.

"Time to move!" you said.

"Can't we kick him a few times while he's down?"

"Bill, can you please…" you said, slipping your left shoulder under his right arm and lifting him to his feet.

His head drooped forward as you navigated him into the garage. "He called June a chink whore."

You winced. "We've got to intercept her before she comes back."

"She's not even Chinese," said Bill.

You lowered him into the back seat. "Just lie down." You carefully removed your shirt with your left hand and offered it to him. "For your head," you said. "It's bleeding."

Bill touched his head and inspected his bloody fingers. "Oh."

"There's a hospital nearby."

His brow furrowed. "What's wrong with your arm?"

"I think I dislocated my shoulder."

The garage opened like a whale's mouth, and the blinding light of day flooded its cavernous belly. Sweat spilled off you like foam down the side of an overfilled pint. You took a right and drove by the lobby at a crawl. Reno was still on the floor, his head held in his hands. Coming directly for you was June, lugging her duffel bag like it contained the entirety of her sordid past—every busted promise, each abandoned dream. You slammed on the brakes, threw the car into park, flipped on the hazards and jumped out.

"Hey. I know. I'm an asshole. I know."

"Get away from me," she said, reaching into her purse and extracting her keys.

"But I need you to get in the car right now, okay?"

She kept going. You reached with your good arm but she swatted it away.

"Don't fucking touch me!"

"June!"

She looked inside and her body went rigid; her fingers, clutching her mass of keys to the homes of failed relationships, repossessed cars, and storage facilities, turned white. Reno stared at the lobby walls like a drunk, awakening from a bender. He spotted her and struggled to his feet.

"June, look." You pointed to Bill in the back seat of the car. She gasped. "Bill's all fucked up. And my shoulder."

She looked at your arm and brought her hand to her mouth. Reno opened the lobby door and stepped outside, one hand clutching his head. You took a step back and held up your palm, signaling him to stop.

"Enough!" you said. "Back the fuck off!"

"You're fucked, Josh."

"Reno, stop!" said June, as though she were reprimanding an aggressive dog. "Just stop." She faced you and took your good hand. "Go to the hospital," she said. "I can't do this to you anymore."

Reno took another shaky step closer.

"Hold it!" you yelled. "No more of this shit! I just want to get my friend out of here."

Reno stopped on the grass between the building and the sidewalk, about fifteen feet from June. "Fuck the both you. I'm here for my girlfriend."

Your lip quivered. "You don't get to call her that anymore."

"Josh," he smiled, savoring his rage. "I swear, dude. One more word and I'll break your fucking arm."

You looked at her. "I'm sorry…for what I said before. It wasn't…it's not true."

Thick, bulging veins on the side of Reno's neck turned purple. "Baby, you're gonna talk to me right now or I'm not responsible for what happens!"

She removed her sunglasses. Her face was pale but her eyes, strong and steady, focused on yours and didn't waver. She touched your arm.

You felt the tears coming but this was no moment to show weakness. So you did the only thing you could to stop yourself from crying—you turned your grief into anger, anger at yourself for being no better than him, anger at her for finding her composure in this torrential shitstorm.

"We're going to the hospital," you said.

"That's good," she said. She bent down and spoke through the car's open window. "I'm so sorry, Bill."

"I'm sorry your ex is a racist scumbag."

"Liar!" screamed Reno. "Shut your bald ass up!"

June whirled around. "Reno!"

"My head hurts, baby," he whined. "Josh cheapshotted me."

You grasped her wrist. "I can't just leave you."

She touched your cheek. "This is my problem, baby, not yours."

Surreal didn't begin to describe the moment. Suddenly you were Ingrid Bergman at the end of *Casablanca*, and June was putting you on a path to a better life.

"You're wrong," you said. She sighed deeply. You whispered, "Say goodbye to me, I'll get in the car, put it in drive and then you hop in."

Reno flexed his muscles and cracked his neck. "Five more seconds and we're fighting."

You held her slender fingers. "You don't deserve this!"

"Five!"

You tightened your grip. "All this time, everything we've been through…it can't be for nothing."

She smiled sadly, like she was looking at a memory of a person. "Four!"

"Go," she said.

"Three!"

"Jesus, give it a fucking rest, man!" you shouted, your voice quivering. "It's over, all right? We're leaving."

You got into your stuffy car, your slippery, quaking palm barely able to grip the steering wheel. June headed towards Reno and he held out his hands. You drove fast, filling your ringing ears with wind.

Sprawled across the back seat, Bill oozed sweat onto the upholstery and blood onto your tee shirt. "I take it you were joking about the hospital."

"No."

"Well I don't have insurance. Do you?"

You hesitated. "Kind of."

"Does 'kind of' insurance cover ER visits?"

"I don't know. Fuck."

You contemplated going to your parents' house. But there was no hiding what had happened here. You'd been in a fight; you'd sustained moderate injuries; you needed urgent care. And mother grizzlies had nothing on your dad—little matter that you were a grown man now. Your mom would try to calm him down, tell him to listen, breathe, keep a level head while you explained what had happened. After all, no one was seriously injured. And then you'd have to tell them what you'd been hiding for the past three weeks: June was back in your life. That fragile image of you that they'd held in their heads for the past few months—an adult with a respectable job that they could trust to continue making good decisions—would crumble in their fingers like an arid clump of dirt.

You swerved into the 7-Eleven parking lot, empty again save for the silver hatchback with the bolt welded to its door. "I'm getting you some ice."

"I can walk," said Bill.

"Just stay here, man."

"The Wizard used to be a nurse. He can examine me. Besides, I'm fucking starving."

"Really?"

"I'm so fucking hungry I could eat a 7-Eleven hot dog."

"I meant about The Wizard."

"That's what he said." Bill carefully peeled the tee shirt from his scalp. "This stop bleeding?"

You looked closely at the wound. It wasn't too deep, more of a scratch than a cut. Even you could tell it wouldn't require stitches. "Yeah, but, what about your eye? Or your fucking brain? You could have a concussion."

"Nothing a chili dog can't fix."

You laughed. He handed you the bloody shirt and you gingerly slipped it on, guilt roiling your belly for having enjoyed a moment of levity. "Fucking June," you said.

"Yeah."

"What the fuck happened?"

"I don't know," said Bill. "You said her family was all fucked up, right? Her dad died when she was really young and..."

"I mean, what happened with Reno? How did you come to have your head wedged in his armpit?"

Bill's lip curled in disgust. "That fucking troglodyte pounded on your intercom for like five minutes. I told him I didn't know who the fuck he was talking about but he didn't buy it."

"Why the hell did you go downstairs?"

"I told you. He called her a chink whore."

"And?"

"And I was like, how often do I get the chance to encounter real evil? I mean, you read about, you see it on the TV, but how often do you get to see it in the flesh? I was sitting in your apartment, doing jack shit like every other day of my useless fucking life, and then Reno drops into my little sheltered world: a bona fide racist woman beater. He's like a fucking lunar eclipse. You know if you look too long it'll burn the back of your retinas but you can't help taking a peek."

"I can't believe I left her with him," you mumbled.

"So I went downstairs. He didn't know who I was so he asked me to let him in and I wouldn't." A smile spread over his swollen face. "And then he must have put two and two together because his face got all red and he told me to fuck off, so I did like, a monkey dance in front of the windows."

You laughed; you couldn't help it. "Ouch," you said, holding your aching shoulder. "Fuck that hurts. Why did you dance?"

"I don't know. He was so fucking confused. Then I started like whooping and screeching like a monkey and I mimed throwing feces at him."

Laughter radiated pain down your arm. "Stop!" you said. "Stop it!"

"Then the elevator opened and before I knew it, your neighbor lady, the one who carries around that rat-faced chihuahua in her purse, walked right past me and straight out the front door."

"Why didn't you run?"

"I did! I ran! They must have bought that fucking elevator from an old folks home! The fucking doors are programmed for people with walkers and hip replacements. My grandpa can make it down the first base line faster than those doors close."

You laughed until tears streamed down your face, pain piercing deeper with each gasp. Bill's swollen face glowed.

"Jesus," you said. "Oh, Jesus what a mess."

"Let's go inside. The Wizard will fix us."

You followed him, the two of you smiling like idiots despite the pain caused by your respective injuries. Stationed beneath the monitor, The Wizard and Amare munched mini donuts and watched the Lotto monitor, their sparse facial hair gone white with powdered sugar. Amare saw you first. He blinked and choked on a wad of dough.

"You missed all the fun," you said, heading for the frozen food section and locating an ancient bag of peas.

"The fuck happened?" said Amare.

At the register, you handed the bag to a visibly flustered Habib. "You have blood," said Habib, scanning the peas and nodding at your shirt.

"It's his," you said, pointing at Bill with your good arm.

"June's psychotic ex showed up," said Bill. "Hey." He motioned to the donuts. "Give me one of those things, will ya?" Amare handed Bill a bite-sized donut and Bill popped it in his mouth. He sighed. "Violence makes me fucking starving."

You handed the peas to Bill. "Put this on your eye."

He pressed the frozen bag against the swelling. "How long have these been in there?"

"Frozen vegetables are not our number one best seller," said Habib.

"This feels like a frozen geode."

Habib emerged from behind the register, took the peas from Bill and smacked them a few times on the counter, breaking apart the frozen mass. "Here," he said, handing them back. He turned toward Amare. "You must take him to a hospital."

"Who?" you and Bill said in unison.

Habib pointed at you. "That shoulder is separated. It must be put back in its place."

You felt hot breath on your neck and turned to see The Wizard, his head tilted in absorption, his massive hands hovering just above your shoulder. You stepped away.

"What are you doing?"

"It's a subluxation. Your humerus is only partially out of its socket. Would you like me to put it back for you?"

"No," said Habib, coming out from behind the register. "Without an X-ray there is no way to tell if the ligaments have been damaged. Josh," he said, touching your good shoulder and looking you in the eye. "Have you separated this shoulder before?"

You shook your head no.

"Habib," said The Wizard, "I know that you are a man of great learning, but I assure you, this is a trifling injury. I'd wager all the nacho cheese sauce in the Valley on it. This can be resolved without subjecting Josh to the bureaucratic quagmire that is American medicine."

The truth was that you'd been kicked off the family health plan after your last birthday. At present, you were paying fifty bucks a month for a plan that covered a fraction of catastrophic injuries.

"My insurance is garbage," you said. "If I make a claim on it, I lose it forever."

Habib sighed. "I do not understand this health care system."

"American medicine is about as functional as your relationship with June," said Amare.

"No one's relationship is perfect," you said.

"I realize that, but few are so perfectly fucked as yours."

"Cut the guy some slack," said Bill. "He just got in a fight for chrissakes."

"And why was he fighting?" said Amare. "Josh, you're a responsible adult who's a role model to teenagers and your shiftless friends. What the fuck are you doing brawling with your ex-girlfriend's ex-boyfriend?"

Your jaw quivered and pressure swelled in your chest. You glanced around the room, at the assembly of faces waiting for a response to a question that had no reasonable answer. "Bill was getting the shit kicked out of him."

"And why was Bill getting the shit kicked out of him?" Amare looked Bill up and down and shook his head back and forth. "Because of June! Because he's infatuated too and he decided to defend her honor or something by getting in his first ever fistfight!"

"Boys," interjected The Wizard.

Bill grimaced and adjusted the frozen peas. "Ah, excuse me."

"This arguing will not help you," said Habib.

"That was not my first fistfight."

"Habib is right," said the Wizard.

"I punched Billy Livingston in the fourth grade."

"Jesus, Bill," said Amare. "That's not the point."

"He called my sister a bitch so I slugged him. I would've won too if he hadn't bit me. Jaws like a pit bull. I've still got the scars," he said, proffering his furry arm.

The door swung open, the electric bell chimed and two police officers—one tall and trim, who looked to be in his mid-thirties, the other younger, portlier, with meaty arms, no visible neck, and a ruddy complexion—walked inside, boots clomping the laminate floor like hangmen marching across the gallows. They sported crew cuts, dark sunglasses, and, judging by their stiff gait, raging cases of hemorrhoids.

Bill shrank behind the beef jerky display. Amare and The Wizard migrated back to their stations beneath the monitor and dug into their pockets for their Lotto tickets.

"Good afternoon, Officers," said Habib, resuming his post behind the register.

The fat one's sunglassed gaze roamed from you to Bill and back to you. "You guys in some kind of accident?"

The trim one kept his eyes on you as he plucked a smoothie from rows of refrigerated drinks. He nodded at your injury. "That shoulder looks like it's seen better days."

You felt the color drain from your face. "I fell off my bike."

"Yeah?" the fat one said. He craned his neck to get a better view of Bill. "You land on this guy's face?"

"Why do you not tell them?" said Habib. "These two," he continued, gesturing to you and Bill. "They were victims of an assault."

The fat one lowered his shades to the bridge of his nose. "That true?" You pictured him practicing this face in front of the mirror, eliciting imaginary homicide confessions.

"No, no, no," you said. "He misunderstood. It was a bike accident. I just said that I *felt* like I'd been in a fight."

The trim officer broke the seal on his smoothie. He sighed and stood by the register, his boredom giving him an air of experience, as though he'd seen enough to know what kind of policing would bring accolades and what kind would bring paperwork. The fat one wasn't satisfied. He turned and looked out the front window.

"Where's your bike now?" he said.

The trim one scrutinized Amare and The Wizard. "Hey, big man. I've seen you in here before, right?"

The Wizard smiled and nodded. "It is eminently possible, Officer."

"Sure I have. Always stationed right there, playing the Lotto. Who's your friend?"

The Wizard glanced at Amare. "Perhaps you should ask him?"

"What's your name, fella?"

Amare smirked.

The fat cop frowned and took a couple steps toward Amare, his ruddy cheeks further reddening, his blond eyebrows forming a truculent V. "Hey homeboy. My partner asked what your name was. This is where you answer him."

Amare sighed. "Amare."

"Stoudemire?" said the fat cop, chuckling.

"Ha. No. That's a funny observation though. Because Amar'e Stoudemire and I do share a first name. That's funny."

The fat cop's mouth hung open while he tried to figure out if he was being insulted.

"You can cut the sarcasm now, fella," said the trim cop.

"Hussein," said Amare, fishing out a mini donut and plopping it in his mouth. "My name's Amare Hussein."

The fat cop put his hands on his hips. "What, are you kidding me?"

"Why?" said Amare. "Is there an NBA player named Hussein too?"

"What do you...don't you read the papers?" said the fat cop. "Or do you just piss away your time playing the Lotto?"

"Who reads the papers anymore?" said Amare.

The fat cop rolled his eyes. "Well if you did..."

"Doyle," the trim cop interjected.

"...you'd know that we're at war. My brother's in Iraq right now, fighting a nation of terrorists led by one of your relatives."

Amare winced. "That sure sucks for your brother."

The trim cop slid his ATM card and punched in his Pin number. "He's pulling your leg, Doyle."

The fat cop tilted his head and looked at Amare. "That true, *Hussein*? You having fun with me?"

"Nope." Amare chuckled. "I promise you," he said, a smile tugging at his lips. "I'm not having any fun."

The fat cop walked within a couple feet of Amare and stared into his eyes. He squinted. "You wouldn't happen to be under the influence of narcotics, would you?"

Amare stiffened. "No, sir."

The fat cop squinted at Amare's eyes. Then he turned his head and addressed the room. "My brother's off fighting jihad, risking his butt to protect our way of life and what does this guy do? He hangs out at 7-Eleven, playing the Lotto."

He turned back in time to catch Amare rolling his eyes.

"Did you just roll your eyes at me?"

"I'm sorry," said Amare, his eyes fixed passively on the floor but his voice strong and steady. "I just wouldn't put it that way... that your little brother is fighting for me."

"Well maybe it's time you woke up and smelled the coffee."

"Dude," Bill harshly whispered.

As Amare met the fat cop's belligerent gaze, his eyes twinkled. "It's just that I don't work for Big Oil or Halliburton is all."

The fat cop straightened his back and hooked his thumbs on his belt. "What the hell does that mean?"

"It means that I don't profit from American imperialism. Quite the opposite in fact."

"Liberal claptrap," snarled the fat cop.

Amare sighed. He looked at the monitor, then at his Lotto ticket; he crumpled it in his fist and tossed it into the garbage. "With all due respect, Officer," said Amare, "you should know whose side you're on."

"Excuse me?"

"It's the same side I'm on, the same one he's on," he said pointing to Habib, "and him and him and him and your brother too."

The fat cop smiled, a light shining in his eyes like he was savoring these last few seconds before he took out his nightstick and demonstrated the difference between the two of them. He pointed an accusatory finger. "I know your kind. You don't have sides, you have opinions. What good are those, huh? You're just talk. You leave the doing to others."

The trim cop strolled toward the door. "C'mon, Doyle."

Amare waited a few beats, pressure mounting, as though he'd covered the nozzle of a running hose with his thumb. "People who think like you make me sad."

The cop crossed his arms over his chest. "Oh yeah?"

Amare cupped his hands in front of him. "You get fed a big bowl of shit, but instead of saying, 'I refuse to eat this shit,' you praise the people who gave it to you and ask for more. Look at your poor brother. He goes halfway across the world and risks his life, and these assholes can't even get their story straight about why he's there."

The fat cop shook his head in vehement disagreement.

Amare said, "Meanwhile, what does our government do? They slash veterans' benefits so they can subsidize oil companies, and give tax breaks to the billionaires who will be counting on you, the police, to protect them from the people when the people finally get fed up with eating shit."

The fat cop's face went from red to violet and his gaze wandered to you. The grimace you'd been wearing had evaporated like water from a wet towel left to dry in the sun. You rubbed your cheeks, dissembling your smile.

With one hand on the door, the trim cop said, "Hey, man of the people, how about you take your friend to a hospital?"

"If that's where he wants to go," said Amare.

"Doyle," the trim cop said, opening the door and triggering the electric chime. The fat cop squinted at Amare and rubbed his chin. "Ronnie!"

"I hope your brother comes home safe, Officer," said Amare. The fat cop took a deep breath, pursed his lips, and nodded. Without uttering another word, he pivoted and headed out the door.

"Jesus Christ," said Bill, emerging from the background, the flaccid bag of peas still pressed against his eye. "You're a fucking lunatic."

Habib came out from behind the counter and frowned at your shoulder. "So you do not use the hospital when you are injured and you do not go to the police when you are beaten. Is this correct?"

"Believe me," said Amare. "These things just turn into accusations and recriminations and in the end, the only winners are the lawyers."

"This is democracy," said Habib.

"This is capitalism," said Amare.

"You're lucky that cop didn't cave in your skull," said Bill.

Amare laughed. "I'll bet that brother of his beat the shit out of him when he was a kid."

Habib took your good arm. "Come sit down." He guided you around the counter to a high stool. The Wizard followed. You took a seat and the Wizard stood behind you, his cannonball belly pressed against your lower back, his nacho cheese and jalapeño-breath on your neck. Gently, he rolled up the sleeve of your shirt. Bill and Amare leaned against the counter and wiped powdered sugar from their fingers onto their shirts, their eyes blazing like naked light bulbs.

"You are sure that you want to do this?" said Habib. "You could risk aggravating the injury. Surgery would be much greater expense than an X-ray."

"I guess so. I don't know."

The Wizard placed a hand on your good shoulder. "Life is a difficult journey to navigate without a little faith in our friends."

"Fuck it," you said. "I trust you, Ozzie."

"Take a deep breath," he said.

You sucked air into the deepest recesses of your lungs, corners you imagined untouched by nicotine, smog, and stress, traces of vibrant pink tissue that would one day spread across blackened terrain, rejuvenating damage and decay wrought by pollution, cigarettes, and the fragile self-image of a diffident teenager that inspired you to take up such a nasty habit in the first place.

"Exhale."

You blew out and a flash of white—instantaneous and searing, like an electric shock or the first time June smiled at you—eclipsed the faces of your friends. And then, just like that, you were back, repaired to your imperfect self.

"You okay?" said Bill.

"I think so." You tested your arm. It was sore, but you could move it.

"From the clutches of sin and Satan," intoned the Wizard.

You put your hand on the Wizard's meaty shoulder. "Thank you."

Habib instructed you to perform a few basic motions and then, satisfied that all was well, he retrieved an old tee shirt from the back, and constructed a makeshift sling.

"If the pain gets worse, you must promise to have an X-ray taken."

You tried to answer. All you wanted to say was that you understood, that you were grateful for their help, but you couldn't. There was a lump in your throat the size of a lemon. Your eyes filled with water and you ground your teeth, unable to accept that you were again fighting tears. It was crazy. You weren't a crier. You handled adversity with equanimity and aplomb…occasionally with alcohol. But in that moment, as your gratitude and shame centers converged, you found you could not speak. So you sat there, breathing heavily, the lies you'd fed yourself about being able to hack this alone echoing back at you from the towering edifice with which they'd collided.

The Wizard placed a giant palm in the center of your back and your breathing steadied. You rubbed the tears from your eyes before they had a chance to escape and inhaled a sour, fetid odor. You sniffed your armpit.

"I reek," you said.

"It is okay," said Habib. "You are in a convenience store. I pass gas in here all the time. No one notices."

"Ha!" laughed Bill. "That's the best thing I've heard all day."

Habib nodded. "Thank you."

"Gentleman," said the Wizard, waddling toward the door. Dimmed was the prideful glow that had just brightened his unshaven face. His cheeks sagged like a discarded rubber mask and his complexion was the grey of collected ash. "All this excitement has suddenly taken its toll."

You stepped in his path and stuck out your hand; your slim fingers disappeared inside his fleshy paw.

"Thank you for reaffirming my belief in the kindness of strangers."

"We are strangers no longer, Joshua." A childish smile of readily accepted praise tugged at the corners of his mouth. He lumbered through the doors, the electric chime rang, and a cool breeze blew inside. You skin, sticky with dried sweat and flecked with burgundy droplets of Bill's blood, felt reptilian, desiccated, toughened by the harsh elements to which you'd suddenly become acclimated. A middle-aged man in a grey pinstripe suit entered, paused at the threshold like a traveler who has returned home to find his furniture rearranged. Then, satisfied that whatever had just transpired would not impact him, he headed toward the Slurpee machine.

"See you soon, Habib," you said.

"A hot bath and then ice, my friend. It is the doctor's orders."

*

YOU SANK INTO THE tub. Images and conversation fragments swirled around in your head like water vapor: your promise to June's dying mother, the weightless, brittle bones of her feeble hand; an assurance made to your own mom over coffee and zucchini bread that you knew what was good for you, that you wouldn't allow your life to take a back seat to someone else's drama; Bill and Amare's foul and decrepit hostel, your insistence that they spend a few nights at your place; their gratitude, the rounds of whiskey and gingers imbibed at The Burrow that first celebratory night; long nights of communal sleep, four people without a wall between them and the honesty of sound, sight, and smell that was the natural outcropping of such an arrangement. You tried to discern a story, place yourself, this moment, in some kind of narrative arc. But stories are never discrete. They start long before the beginning and reverberate long after the end—aftershocks, alerting generation after generation to structural vulnerabilities they either forgot about or were ignorant of all along. In all likelihood, none of this would make sense until the precise moment, years later, in which you found yourself a player in a similar story.

A few short weeks ago, you had seen your small gains—your job, your relationship to your students, your inclination to help friends in need—as evidence of a page turned; triumphs over the memory of a failed relationship. But that viewpoint was unsustainable as long as June was still in your life. Viewed through a different lens, you weren't so sure that triumph was what you were after anyway. Its implications—that the trials you had endured brought you no closer to enlightenment or peace; that time, youth, and energy had spilled from a glass that could never be refilled; that despite signs of progress, you had merely drifted further from her, further from yourself, further from love—terrified you. Your mother used to say, "You are exactly where you're supposed to be." But you'd been here before—June with Reno; you left shouldering a duffel bag of guilt. In your experience, guilt was the only habit tougher than smoking to quit.

A key rattled in the apartment door. Your listened to it open and close. A moment later, keys clattered on a hard surface. Footsteps crossed the carpet like a soft patter of spring rain and stopped outside the bathroom door. There were three light knocks—she wasn't taking time to gather herself, wasn't deviating from a course that had been charted before entering the apartment.

"Are you in there?" she said.

"I'm in the bath."

"Can I come in?"

"Of course."

She entered with bowed head and averted eyes. She lowered the toilet seat cover and sat, her black hair serving as a blinder to your nakedness, as though there were one square inch of your flesh that she hadn't thoroughly investigated.

It occurred to you that the reason she was hiding her face might have nothing at all to do with modesty. You sat up quickly, sloshing about lukewarm bathwater.

"Show me your face," you said. She brushed her hair aside and looked you in the eyes. There were no marks. "Did he hurt you?"

She shook her head.

"Are you sure?"

"Your shoulder looks better," she said. She reached out but her hand stopped halfway. "Is it…is it okay now?"

"Forget about my shoulder. It's fine. How did you get away?"

"It wasn't like that."

"He let you go?"

"What about Bill?" she said, holding her breath, picking at a rough edge of fingernail.

"Bill's fine," you said. She exhaled. "His low expectations have made him one of the most resilient people I know." She smiled and shook her head in that way that suggested your sense of humor required a certain kind of tolerance that you were lucky she possessed. "To be honest, I think the whole experience energized him."

"Stop it," she said, her smile widening.

You sat up and pulled your legs to your chest. "You wanna get in here?"

She shook her head. "No thanks."

"C'mon. A little naked time with Joshy. I'll add some hot water."

She bit her nails. "I don't think that would be right."

"Baby."

"Please," she said.

The flush in her cheeks, her sudden shallowness of breath betrayed the bend of her resolve, her desire to succumb. You stroked her arm and your wet fingertips trailed glistening streaks across her olive skin like dew droplets down a leaf.

"Ba-by," you cooed.

She pulled her arm away. "Stop."

That stung, the finality of it. Not to mention the irony that at this point in your story, she would be the one to say no.

"Can you hand me a towel please?" You wanted out of the bath. You felt trapped—wet, naked, and rejected.

"Of course."

She removed the towel from the hook on the back of the door and you stood up in the tub, dripping, exposed, daring her to avert her eyes again. She met your gaze and handed it over. No false modesty, no shame, no fear. Once again you resented her composure, resented her for demonstrating the kind of growth that had never happened when you'd both been in the habit of saying yes to one another. It felt like she'd anticipated this exact scenario, like she'd made a promise to herself and was in the process of sticking to it. The thought that she had made resolutions regarding how she would handle you was almost too much to bear.

You wrapped the towel around your waist. "You want to give me a minute here?"

She left the bathroom and you dried in the aftermath of her rebuff. You exited the bathroom, drew the curtain between the bedroom area and the living/dining room area and dressed in the dark while she pick-picked at those nails of hers and quietly cleared her throat once, twice, a third time. You got dressed, parted the curtain, sat on the bed, and scanned the room.

"Where's your duffel bag?" you said.

"I'm staying with my sister for a little while."

"April?"

"Nope. Dolores." She dug into her purse and pulled out a pack of cigarettes.

You tried to mask your joy, but it was hard. You'd waited for this moment for a long time—for an adult with no ulterior motives to take on the mantle of June's caretaker. You'd hoped an invitation might be made at June's mom's funeral, but June had taken issue with the way Dolores had handled the arrangements and bailed early.

"That's good," you said. "I'm glad."

"I figured you would be." She lit a cigarette. Considering that this might be the last time you saw her for a while, you decided against giving her any grief for smoking inside. You got a saucer from the cupboard, sank into the sofa, and placed it on the cushion between you. You leaned back, your damp hair slick against the faux leather, and watched tendrils of smoke curl towards the ceiling and form a blue cloud.

"Where's she living these days?"

"Culver City."

"That's far."

She took a drag and stubbed out the half-smoked cigarette. You got up, opened the door to the balcony in time to see Bill approach the building and disappear under the lobby's green awning.

"Bill's home."

Her face blanched. "I should go." She stood, slipping her purse strap over her shoulder, and headed for the door.

"June." You reached out and caught her elbow.

"What?" Her eyes pleaded with you to let her go.

You didn't have an answer. You couldn't say what you felt: *Now that you have somewhere else to go, I'm not so sure I want you to leave.*

She removed your hand from her elbow, squeezed your fingers and then dropped them. "Dolores is picking me up on the corner. I just wanted to make sure you guys were okay."

"When will I see you again?"

"Josh."

"What?"

She kissed you on the mouth, her lips slightly parting like a first cautious kiss between lovers. A spare key rattled in the doorknob, she pulled away and the door swung open. Bill froze like a deer caught in headlights, the mouse over his eye reduced in size but still an angry shade of red.

"Sorry," he said.

"Hey Bill," said June.

"I can come back later."

You nodded, eager to accept his offer but she said, "Don't!" and slipped past him into the hallway. "I was on my way out anyway." She touched his forearm. "I'm glad you're okay. I'm sorry I caused so much trouble."

"It wasn't your fault," said Bill. "I started it."

June backed through the doorway. "Like I said."

"June," you said. She glanced toward the elevator, bit her lower lip. "Don't be a stranger." She smiled at you as though you'd said the right thing and that made you feel even worse—that such a rare person would be satisfied with such a lame cliché.

Then she walked away.

Self-loathing followed you back inside like an obedient dog. Bill opened two beers and put one in your hand. "Drink it."

You did as you were told. A minute or so later the intercom buzzed; you ran to it and pressed the talk button, ready to promise her the world, grant any request. All you'd wanted from her was evidence that you were more than a life raft in a series of life rafts that she clung to until they were punctured too full of holes to float.

"June?"

For a moment there was no response, just street sounds and static.

"Uhm, it's me," said Amare. "I forgot my key."

"Oh. C'mon up." You buzzed him in and faced Bill, who was suddenly preoccupied by the task of peeling a beer bottle label—a gesture you guessed was meant to spare you the embarrassment of a witness to the unmistakable note of need in your voice when you called out her name.

*

THAT NIGHT THE THREE of you retreated to The Burrow. Having earlier discovered a check from his parents in your mailbox, Bill quickly got drunk on bourbon and beer and then bounced a dart off the side of the electronic dartboard into a petite blonde girl's cheek. He tried to apologize by buying a round for her and her boyfriend, but the boyfriend wasn't having it. With a firmly extended arm, he barred Bill from getting too close to the girl, eyeing you and Amare all the while. In the past, you would have intervened on Bill's behalf, but that night you didn't have the stomach to reason with aggressive boyfriends in the mood to exhibit their quick tempers. You held your darts in one hand, a whiskey and ginger in the other and leaned against the popcorn machine, waiting for the boyfriend to finish demonstrating his physical dominance to all the lecherous eyes, sparkling in anticipation of violence. Maybe Bill's bruised face had given the boyfriend the impression that he was looking for a fight, but Bill's demeanor—his bowed head, sagging eyelids, and slurred apologies—eventually convinced him otherwise.

Harrison showed up around eleven. You abandoned the darts and the four of you snagged a booth from a group of yuppie thirty-somethings that had no business being there in the first place and had filled the jukebox with a bunch of tired eighties rock anthems, imagining that there was something charming or original about drunkenly reciting the lyrics to Bon Jovi's *Living on a Prayer*. You slid across the seat, catching your jeans on a grimy piece of electrical tape meant to hold together a tear in the vinyl. Amare got in beside you and gazed indifferently at the television hanging over the bar. Harrison scooted in across from you. Bill flopped down next to him and stared into his drink. Amare and Bill had hung out with Harrison a few times, but always as part of a crew. As you recounted the day's events to Harrison, the boys stayed quiet, as though, embarrassed by having intruded on friends who had gotten together by choice, they were trying to make themselves invisible.

"You okay?" said Harrison. Until that moment, you hadn't realized how badly you'd needed someone to ask you that question.

"It feels weird to lose her again, even if I didn't really want her back in the first place."

Harrison sipped his glass of Baker's and nodded. "Sure."

"At least this time she's safe."

"She's…June," slurred Bill. He squinted at Harrison through bloodshot eyes. "You know June?"

"Oh yeah," chuckled Harrison. "I know June."

"She's…" Bill clutched Harrison's elbow. "Isn't she pretty?"

Harrison laughed. "Yeah. She's pretty all right."

"Damn right she is," said Bill, patting Harrison on the shoulder and returning his hand to his drink. "How Josh ever… I could never talk to a girl like that."

"She's with her older sister now," you said. "Dolores. She's solid. I wish June had gone there months ago."

"Sometimes that makes it harder," said Harrison. "When the person is solid, I mean."

"How's that?" you said.

"Cause of the contrast. She doesn't want every solid person in her life thinking she's a fuck up."

You downed the rest of your drink and chewed on a mouthful of ice. An old Tom Waits song came on the jukebox and everything got quiet, as though the bar and its patrons had suffered a simultaneous gut punch.

"Who the hell puts Tom Waits on before one-thirty in the morning?" said Harrison. "I came here to feel good." You smiled. "This was you, wasn't it? You morose son of a bitch."

You held up your right palm. "Not guilty." You craned your neck and spied a short, curvaceous brunette, leaning against the jukebox and singing along with the lyrics. Her eyes were closed; a bottle of PBR dangled loosely from her fingers. You nodded in her direction and Harrison looked over his shoulder.

"Somebody's gotta do something."

Bill lifted his face up from the table and openly ogled the girl. "I'm buying her a drink." And before you could stop him, he was off, stumbling his way toward the bar.

"Is June's sister married?" said Amare, his eyes fixed on the stained glass window near the ceiling.

"No," you said. "Why?"

"So that was her boyfriend that picked her up?"

"What are you talking about?"

Amare gazed down into his drink.

"Jesus Christ," you said, your breath grew shallow and your hands trembled.

"Take it easy," said Harrison.

"A guy picked her up?" you said.

Amare nodded.

You quelled an impulse to throw your drink at the wall.

"What did he look like?"

"I didn't..."

"Did he have sideburns and tattoos? Was he more Rockabilly or more yuppie? What fucking kind of car was he driving?"

"I don't know exactly." He sipped his drink and leaned back. "It was black. Looked like an old Chevy."

You groaned. Tom Waits lamented a lost love over the speakers, goading you to find the nearest gutter and lay down your weary head in a puddle.

"Let me out," you said.

"Josh," said Harrison.

"Seriously," you said. "I just need some air."

Amare stood and you slid out of the booth. You made for the exit, weaving through the hipsters and the drunks, past the giant doorman perched on his reinforced steel stool beside the door.

"Hey, homey," he said. "You gonna be sick, go around the side."

You burst through the exit, nearly toppling a young couple on their way inside. "Sorry," you mumbled, but the guy still had to squint maliciously at you, as though you'd intended to harm whoever stood on the other side of that door.

You clenched your fists. "You got a fucking problem, then say it!"

The guy put his hands up. The girl's eyes widened and her jaw dropped.

You took a deep breath. "Fuck me. I'm sorry."

The girl stepped behind the guy and pointed at you. "You *should* be sorry. We didn't *do* anything."

The guy grinned. He stood up a little straighter, puffed out his chest. "You're lucky I'm a tolerant guy, buddy."

You grimaced. "Look, I apologized precisely so you wouldn't go and say something stupid like that."

"What the fuck?"

Ordinarily, the adrenaline rush accompanying the kind of threat you were about to make would cause your hands to quiver, but the combination of booze and fury made the finger you pointed at the guy as straight and steady as a baseball bat. "You call me 'buddy' again and we're fighting." You lowered your hand and watched his eyes, waiting for them to give away his intent.

The girl tugged at the sleeve of the guy's flannel. "C'mon, baby. This guy's an asshole."

He held your gaze for another second or two and then broke. "Only because she's here, motherfucker," he said.

You snorted.

He shot you one last murderous glance and walked inside.

You fished your cigarettes out of your pocket, shook one free of the pack. As you inhaled that first deep drag, you leaned against the wall, lumpy red brick boring into the back of your skull. The night was cool, the temperature having dipped significantly since you'd arrived. The clench went out of your muscles and you sat there like a doused campfire, wisps of white smoke rising from your impotent sizzle.

Harrison walked outside and looked both ways, his eyes passing over you like a shrub, a newspaper vending machine, or some such static piece of scenery.

"Hey," you said.

He flinched. "Jesus!"

"I'm fine," you said. "No pep talk, okay?"

"Bullshit you're fine." He fished into his pockets, pulled out a decimated cigarette pack and shook it. "Give me one of those things," he said, crumpling the empty pack and tossing it in the ashtray.

"I just wanted a humdrum life for a while. You know…go to work, come home, crack a beer, watch baseball, and not worry about anything besides the Sox's playoff chances."

"What's the worst case scenario here?" he said.

You sighed. "History repeats itself."

"In which case she'll come crawling back, right?"

"And then the whole fucking circus starts all over again."

"Well now, that's up to you, not her."

You groaned. "This is so boring." You flicked your half-smoked cigarette into the street, where its tip glowed amidst an armada of tires. "I hate these conversations. I'm sure that's hard for you to believe, but they're really like my least favorite thing."

"Man, as long as you chase wounded birds, you're doomed to repeat this conversation."

You sank back into the brick.

"Stop looking so sad," he said. "That's step one. If you stop sighing and frowning so fucking much, you'll attract a different kind of person, the kind of person who'll make you want to smile like an idiot all the time. Then you can spend idle evenings with friends talking about baseball or books like you used to."

Amare walked outside and approached the two of you. "Can I get one of those things?"

"Since when do you smoke?"

"I'm sorry, dude," he said, putting a hand on your shoulder. "I should have kept my mouth shut."

"Forget it." You gave him a cigarette and lit if for him. He took a drag, held the smoke in his mouth and let it dribble out in a thick, un-inhaled rope. "Better that I find out now."

Harrison put his cigarette out on the sole of his shoe. "How's your boy Bill doing in there?"

"Still talking up that girl," said Amare.

"No shit?" said Harrison.

"Who's holding down our table?" you said.

"Long gone. As soon as I stood up, some vultures swooped on it like a fresh carcass. Didn't even bother to clear off the empties."

"Fuck it," you said, remembering your near confrontation. "I probably shouldn't go back in there anyway."

Harrison raised an eyebrow. "Why's that?"

You shook your head back and forth, indicating that it wasn't worth getting into.

He shrugged and suggested that the four of you head to another bar, but Amare wanted to stick around and wait for Bill. He said Bill had made the girl laugh out loud and the three of you agreed that sounded too promising to interrupt.

"He's such an idiot," said Amare. "Girls love him when he's not insulting them. You have no idea."

"I actually have no trouble believing that," you said.

Harrison put a hand on your shoulder. "Look, seeing that you're not in the mood for speeches and you're too broke to join me in another round of Baker's, maybe you should get a little private time. Go for a drive, go home, take a shower. Do some fucking thing to get your head clear. I'll give your boys a lift home."

"Yeah?"

"Take a breather, dude," said Amare. "Trust me, you won't miss anything."

You loved your friends. The best kind of friends didn't need to hear the sound of their own voices; they weren't gluttons for gossip, or people looking for human dumpsters to unload their own problems into; their purpose was to protect you, to bolster you, to argue in the face of evidence to the contrary that you were right and good and worthy of their loyalty. You handshake-hugged each of them and wandered off, your eyes on your feet, carefully avoiding the cracks in the sidewalk.

You headed for the hills with the windows rolled down, the stereo blasting some wild Ornette Coleman to eradicate the loneliness, bridge the distance between you and the infinite. Some things were still pure, unsullied, uncorrupted. This music belonged to an era in your life that came before the advent of June. She hadn't liked jazz when it was free; the lack of structure made her squirm. You pointed out the irony. You told her that there was redemption in this music if she listened for it, that the cloying pseudo-folk songs she sang along to were nothing more than an anodyne, while this music, unfettered and boundless, manifested revolt, catharsis, renewal. You could see her now, unconvinced but smiling nonetheless at your passionate entreaties. So this music was tied to her in an oblique kind of way after all. Because you'd felt special when she looked at you in that way—that way that let you know you'd been seen. It was a look that lacked any trace of the indifference or suspicion that you'd come to expect from girls. June had been the dawn of positive attention. After her, women started noticing you, both when she was by your side and when she wasn't, as though you'd materialized from some hazy, spectral, timorous suggestion of a man into something desirable.

You crested the canyon and turned onto Mulholland Drive, the serpentine road that wound along the crest of the hills bifurcating the Valley and the city. Once the hub of the drag-racing world, this road possessed memories of cars slashing gaping wounds in the black night as they barreled, side by side, down its two lanes, screaming around blind turns, reaping adrenaline and glory, colliding head-on with unsuspecting motorists or swerving at the last second to avoid the crash and launching off the little lump of dirt along the road's edge to plummet to a fiery death amongst the shrubs and coyotes.

You pulled off the road alongside an empty lookout point—someplace conducive to reflection, to epiphany. This would be the point in the story, you thought, where you'd turn a corner, discover a new path, or recognize that you'd already turned a corner and the new path was there, laid out before you, and all you had to do was put one foot in front of the other. There'd be no need to know where the path led. It was enough that the path was new. History would not repeat itself; your mistakes would not be lived for nothing.

Across the street from where you parked was a house with a security system placard staked in their plush lawn beside a concrete lawn jockey. A yellow Hummer boasting a Bush/Cheney bumper sticker slumbered in the driveway.

You left your car, stepped over the chain meant to deter hooligans from enjoying the seclusion of the lookout spot after dark. A splintered bench beckoned; something rustled the thicket of bushes in front of you. Something will always be rustling the bushes, you thought, and took a seat to watch the tiny cars below—haughty headlights headed nowhere, but with great purpose. To the west, a truck engine roared. The roar morphed into a cantankerous clattering followed by a low hum as the truck shifted gears to take the hairpin turns. Then it hit a straightaway, hiccuped, and whined as it increased its speed, drew closer. A helicopter swooped into view from the east, drowning the sound of the truck, and careened over Ventura Boulevard, shining its spotlight on the 101. A faint peal of sirens reached your ears as a convoy of police cars, twinkling like Christmas lights, strung themselves across the freeway. You marveled at how benign life-and-death speed looked from a distance.

The truck rounded the bend beside the lookout point and flashed its high beams on your back, the bushes, and the pink nose and yellow eyes protruding from the thicket. As quickly as the truck had appeared, it exited, leaving you alone with a cloud of exhaust and the sticky sensation of being watched. You were a city boy. You'd gone to college in a heavily forested area, but you'd never grown accustomed to the presence of wild animals. In four years at school, you'd spotted upwards of seven hundred cougars, ninety-eight percent of which turned out to be foliage and two percent of which were actual critters ranging in size from squirrel to raccoon.

You closed your eyes. The creature rustled the leaves again and then moved on, satisfied that it could continue safely on its way. You leaned forward and warmed your hands with your breath. The weather was changing but the change would likely be temporary. Los Angeles never cooled for long. You endured the ache in your shoulder, your cold hands and feet. Even if revelation wasn't lurking here in the shadows, abandoning the spot too soon felt comparable to denying its possibility. So you waited. Soon your bladder began to pound. Something needed to be done.

You stayed low, crossing the street at a dash, and headed straight for the sleeping suburban tank. The bulk and height of the Hummer shielded you from the house's giant picture widows, as you unzipped your fly and soaked the passenger door with a torrential stream of warm, alcoholic piss.

So you hadn't quite figured out what you stood for. At least you were clear about what you stood against.

*

THE NEXT COUPLE OF weeks passed quietly. With June no longer around, the air was different, as though someone had taken a metaphysical broom and swept the psychic dust particles from the atmosphere, clearing space for daydreams. There were times, not many, when you had the place all to yourself. Inspired by your work with Adrienne, you started to write a play about your freshman year at college. You kept your expectations low, didn't harbor any grand Hollywood illusions. This, to you, was precisely what made it worthwhile.

Life fell into a comfortable rhythm. You read by morning, tutored by afternoon, and wrote by night. You spoke with frequency to your parents and even brought the boys to your folks' house for a family dinner. Having defrosted half the freezer, your dad grilled up monstrous porterhouse steaks while mom baked potatoes and steamed farmer's-market-fresh green beans. Fresh off an interview at Whole Foods that he claimed to have nailed, an energized Bill charmed your mother with amusing anecdotes about about his childhood in Maine and talked Red Sox playoff chances with your dad until you thought they might offer him your old bedroom. Amare added the occasional quip to the conversation but didn't really seem like himself. You wanted to attribute his remoteness to something quietly brewing, an incendiary idea that would spring forth suddenly like Athena, fully formed and warrior-garbed from the head of Zeus. But truthfully, the impression he gave was closer to that of a dying flame.

You avoided dive bars, partly because none of you had the funds and partly because the Monday after June's departure, you'd run out of cigarettes and hadn't bought a new pack. It wasn't planned, but something in its spontaneity gave you the feeling that you had a fighting chance. You'd tried to quit before, but the attention focused on the act of quitting drove you near psychological collapse. The more you prepared, the more people you told, the more daunting it seemed and the more easily you unraveled. This time you were determined to fly under the radar, to keep the seriousness of your intention hidden, to store it in some remote nook or cranny, such as a toe or an earlobe, where your conscious mind didn't venture. No gum, no patch, no prescription medications—that shit was tantamount to getting a handjob from a girl you're trying to breakup with. If either of the boys noticed, they were savvy enough not to comment— even during those first few days, when you carried around the hammer you were pretty sure you weren't going to use but you nonetheless needed to feel in your hands. Little mention was made of June, but every time your phone rang, heads perked up like nervous squirrels, listening carefully to the tone of your voice, to whatever its pitch might betray.

Then, one Thursday morning, as you drank your coffee and Amare read his online news, Bill's phone rang. You grabbed it, checked the number, shook Bill awake, and put the thing in his hand. It was Whole Foods, asking him if he could start that afternoon.

"Okay," he said, sitting upright, still in a fog. "Sure, I can do that." His eyes roamed the scenery in utter bafflement, as though he hadn't woken up in the same position every morning for the past six weeks, and landed on your expectant grin—you'd seen the area code and held your breath. As reality sank in and the day broke free from the tentacles of his dreams, self-worth dawned on Bill's face with the brilliance of a fogless sunrise and his whole body seemed to smile.

"I got a job."

"Well all right," you said. "You deserve it, bud."

"I start this afternoon."

"Fucking-a."

He rubbed the sleep from his eyes. The swelling had gone down by now but his cheekbone still bore a faint purplish streak.

"Can I buy you breakfast?" he said.

"As long as it's not a 7-Eleven hot dog."

He grinned.

"Nicely done, Bill."

*

THE THREE OF YOU went to Loretta's, an unassuming little café tucked into a narrow enclave between the kingdoms of Ralphs and CVS. The outdoor seating, a shaded space that snaked around the side of the restaurant and fed into an alley behind Ventura Boulevard, bloomed with potted plants, bougainvillea, and out-of-work actors. A knee-bucklingly beautiful Latina hostess, with braided hair and a gold tooth that sparkled in the sunlight, nearly leveled you with a smile before sitting you at an umbrella-shaded table near the back.

"This place is righteous," said Amare. "Why haven't we been here like every day?"

You smoothed your napkin across your lap. "Wait till you try the French toast."

Amare leaned back and surveyed the landscape. "Just when I was getting down on this city, you pull this little gem out of your back pocket."

"At least you've got a car," said Bill. "I have no idea how I'm getting to work every day. We've gotta look for an apartment within walking distance."

Amare dug into the pocket of his jeans for his cell phone and kept his eyes on its screen as he said, "You want the car? I'll sell it to you."

"How would you get around?"

He put the phone away and contemplated the gallery of beautiful faces. "If you pay my outstanding parking tickets, it's yours."

The waitress, clearly an aspiring actress or model in a yellow tank top that exposed the silky brown skin of her shoulders, brought menus and coffee. She glided away, her delicate shoulder blades arcing toward the crescent moon tattoo on the nape of her neck.

You caught yourself staring. "The women in this place," you said.

"The women in this city," said Bill.

Amare pushed his menu to the center of the table and sipped his black coffee.

"You're not even gonna look?" you said. "There're some inventive scrambles you might want to check out."

"Eggs Benedict is my diner bellwether."

"You can't sell me your car," said Bill, leaning in, his elbows on the table. "If we move near my work, you'll need it more than I will."

"I'm not sure I'm moving with you," said Amare. Bill frowned. "I'm broke, dude."

Bill leaned forward. "So suck it up and borrow a little more money from your folks. Just enough to hold you over until you find a job."

Amare chuckled. "Not a chance."

The waitress in the yellow tank top, her geniality and grace conveying a confidence as yet undiminished by smarmy agents and unreturned phone calls, materialized at your table.

"What can I get for you boys?" she said.

"Eggs Florentine," said Amare.

"Okay."

"I thought Benedict was the bellwether," you said.

"I decided against it." He patted his belly. "Trying to drop a couple LBs."

A bemused grin tugged at the corners of the waitress' mouth. Amare sipped his coffee stoically, letting her puzzlement brew. She finished taking your orders and walked away, glancing back at Amare and accidentally bumping into a table, knocking a pepper shaker to the ground.

"She wanted you to smile at her," you said.

"So what?"

"She's gorgeous," said Bill.

"She's not interested in me. She wants reassurance is all. I'm not in that business."

Bill rubbed his chin and fiddled with his silverware. You kept your mouth shut, fighting the impulse to debate.

After a short wait, the food arrived and was devoured with a minimum of conversation. Not once in the past month had there been so many pregnant pauses. After the perfunctory Red Sox chatter died down, it was all you could do to not count the number of times Bill and Amare chewed their food before swallowing. At the end of the meal, Bill insisted on picking up the check and you insisted on at least paying the tip. Amare kept quiet, using the toothpick on which an orange slice had been impaled to clean his teeth.

You left Loretta's through the back, emerging from its verdant, greenhouse-like patio onto a scorched alleyway. You walked by the loading dock of a massive CVS and a string of grey stucco apartment buildings, your shoes scraping against loose gravel.

"Your breakfast pass muster?" you said.

"Pretty damn good," said Amare.

You waited for him to elaborate but he didn't say anything more. You let him be.

"Those cinnamon swirls in the French toast are ingenious," said Bill. "You almost need a different name for the dish. It's too good to be called French toast."

"It's pretty memorable," you said.

"I've had less memorable blowjobs."

"You're an idiot," said Amare.

"Don't get me wrong. I'm not saying that a blowjob doesn't have a higher ceiling than French toast. I'm just saying that…"

A shiny black Mercedes, doing about thirty-five mph down the alley, shot past you, spitting gravel at your shins.

"What the fuck?!" you yelled.

"Christ!" said Bill.

"Good blowjobs promote deep, restful sleep and a healthy optimism," said Amare, unfazed by the reckless driver. "The best you can hope for after eating French toast is a swift and painless dump."

"Who doesn't enjoy that?" you said.

"A good dump is a beautiful thing," said Amare. "But no one's jeopardizing the presidency of the United States for one."

The three of you giggled the rest of the way to the car. When the laughter subsided, you tried to maintain the smile beyond its natural lifespan. You groped for something to say that might keep Amare talking but your mind was blank. All you could do was keep smiling like an asshole.

Bill rode shotgun. When you'd gone a few blocks, Amare began shifting around in his seat, turning his head this way and that.

"What's up?" you said.

"Something's making a weird noise."

"It's just my basketball," you said. "I keep forgetting to take it out of the trunk."

Bill caught Amare's eyes in the rearview mirror. "So, like, just so we're clear, you're bailing on me, right?"

Amare sighed.

"That's great," said Bill. "Beautiful timing."

"Man, I've got to figure some shit out. In the meantime, it's not fair to you or Josh for me to keep freeloading."

You stopped at a red light, watched the *Don't Walk* sign flash its warning at the empty crosswalk. "Do you have to leave LA?"

"I don't see what choice I have."

"You want to go back to your folks?" said Bill. "To New Jersey?"

"Look, I love you guys," said Amare. "But when I'm with you, it's too easy to avoid reality. I need to inject a little urgency into my days."

"And you're gonna find urgency in Jersey?" said Bill.

"There's no avoiding it in my parents' house."

The light changed. You made a left and drove down your street, a contemplative quiet having descended on the car. You pulled up to the curb to let Amare out but he just sat there.

"I'm afraid of what will happen to me if I stay here."

"You can't sit on your ass forever," you said.

You and Bill pivoted in your seats. Amare stared out the window.

"I can't just get a job with some soul-sucking corporation."

"Like me?" said Bill.

"No offense," said Amare.

"'No offense' he says."

"To tell you the truth, this place scares me. Everything here is centered around the entertainment industry, and I refuse to end up selling my soul to the biggest purveyors of the American myth on the planet."

Bill groaned, but instead of getting angry, Amare's features softened. He smiled, fiddled with his keychain. "Dude, look. I can see it so clearly. I take some bullshit job that I hate just so I can spend my days off in coffee houses, pounding out a screenplay, and I fucking die inside. I'll be like all the other sad sacks in this town that don't even know they're dead, that think that writing a screenplay about the alienation they felt as a teenager makes them vital."

"*Alien Nation*," mumbled Bill. "Now that was a movie. James Caan at the peak of his powers."

Amare opened the door but didn't step out. He chuckled. "That was a pretty fucking good movie." A pleasant breeze swept the stifle from the air. For a minute, the three of you sat there in silence, Amare's words sinking in somewhere deep, nuzzling up against the bone.

He said, "Last week, I wrote a treatment about a serial-killer studio executive who murders screenwriters in the precise way that the killers the screenwriters invented murdered people. And the worst part is, for a few hours, I felt good about myself. Like I'd done something productive with my day." He laughed, got out of the car, took a few steps toward the apartment building, stopped, and turned back. "Anyway…have a great first day ripping off yuppies, Bill."

"Awesome," said Bill. "Thanks for the pep talk."

"I'm fucking with you. Good luck."

Bill nodded and stared through windshield at your clean, tree-lined street. "Let's roll. Time to report to my corporate overlords."

*

BY 4:30 THE HOMEWORK Club was teeming with teenagers, cramming for their first big tests of the semester.

Sophie crashed through the door, still flushed and damp from swim practice. "Josh! I need you!"

You dug your head out of the history textbook you'd been frantically scanning in an attempt to quickly glean everything you'd forgotten about the Magna Carta, without revealing to your new student, Rafi, that you didn't know what the hell you were talking about.

"Nice to see you too, Sophie," you said. "I'll be with you in about twenty."

"Ugh!" she exclaimed. She dropped her heavy book bag into the chair next to you. "This is my seat," she announced to the room. "I'm just going next door for some fries. No one else gets Josh before me." Gazelle-like, she strode out the front door.

Rafi, a distractible fifteen-year-old boy whose long yellow hair had egregiously split ends and who never stopped bouncing his legs or gnawing on his pencils, stared after her.

"Does she like you or something?" he said.

"No."

"She sure acts like it."

"She acts that way with all the boys."

"You're not a boy."

"Here," you said, thrusting the open book in front of him and pointing to its pages. "Read the stuff about Lord Denning. He knew more about the Magna Carta than I ever will."

Obediently, Rafi leaned over the book and tracked the text with his pencil, underlining every single word on the page.

Eric emerged from his office, pushed his glasses up his nose and ensnared you with a meaningful nod. You got up and traversed the familiar olfactory ménage of perfume, bubble gum, and a recently smoked cigarette. You were rapidly approaching three smoke-free weeks, hallowed territory on which you'd never set foot during your previous attempts at quitting.

Eric closed the office door behind you.

"Have a seat, Josh."

Already lowered into a folding chair, the only thing this suggestion did was put you on your guard.

Tim offered an apologetic smile as Eric sat down and tied back his hair in a ponytail with a rubber band. "Adrienne says that you've been a big help with the acting stuff."

Tim leaned forward, belly folds hanging over his belt. "Actually, there have been a number of other students' parents that have called us recently to say that their kids really enjoy working with you."

You bowed your head and focused on a yellow stain on the carpet. "Adrienne's a special kid. All I have to do is show up."

"Adrienne's a pain in the ass," said Eric. "But she's a cash cow. Do you realize how much money her parents spend to send her here every day?"

You sat up straight, lifted your gaze from the ground, and looked at Tim to gauge how comfortable he was with this characterization. Tim didn't say a word, just watched Eric and chewed on his thumbnail.

"Must be a lot," you said.

"Forget it," said Tim. "We didn't call you in here to talk about Adrienne. We wanted to talk to you because Haley Joel has a big shoot coming up. Eric is going to have to be on set five days a week for three months."

"At least," said Eric, reclining in his chair and resting his hands on his belly.

Haley Joel Osmont, child actor from *The Sixth Sense*, was Eric's not-so-secret celebrity client. Since the law required that child actors get the same amount of schooling as other children, when Haley Joel was shooting a movie, Eric administered three hours of grade-appropriate curriculum per day. It was almost enough to make you pity the fifteen-year-old movie star—the idea of getting a break from work only to find Eric waiting in your trailer with a protractor in one hand and your leftover ham and cheese croissant in the other.

Tim said, "We thought that maybe we could pull you out of the study room in his absence, let you take on Eric's other private clients until he gets back."

"Except the higher math and science ones," said Eric. "Tim would absorb those kids because you just don't have the credentials."

"What about the study room kids?" you said.

"We've got other people that can step in and do that work. It hardly qualifies as tutoring anyway, right? All you're really doing in there is keeping them on task."

"It's more than that," said Tim.

"Well," said Eric. "It certainly helps pay the rent."

"How much would I make as a private tutor?" you said.

"More," said Eric, a sloppy grin spreading across his face.

"What happens when you come back?"

"Listen," said Tim. "It would really help us out if you did this. We don't want to lose any of Eric's students and we think that if it's you that steps in for him, there's a good chance we can retain all of 'em."

"I get it," you said. "But I want to know what happens when Eric's job is done. Do I just go back to the study room?"

"We can figure out what happens in a few months in a few months," said Tim.

"Don't worry about it now," said Eric. "Just take the extra money, right?"

You took a deep breath and reclined in the metal chair. They raised their eyebrows and leaned forward. There was no good reason to refuse their offer, but the promotion would be temporary. The prospect of getting ahead, just to be moved back, depressed you. It seemed like just the kind of thing that kept Amare from leaving the house.

You nodded. Tim shook your hand; Eric patted your back.

"Thanks, guys," you said. "For the vote of confidence."

"You're a good tutor," said Tim.

"It's true," said Eric. "Just don't get too friendly with Sophie and everything will be fine." He laughed at his joke and smacked you on the back. Tim scratched his bald spot and looked at the floor.

"Why'd you say that?" you said.

"I was kidding."

You took a deep breath. "Being friends with these kids is very different from 'being friendly.'"

"I don't mean with someone like Adrienne," he said. "Go ahead and be friends with the weird ones who need a little self-esteem boost. It's just that Sophie's a different animal, you know? One of those women whose sole mission on earth is to drive men crazy."

You winced, turned away, and reached for the cool brass doorknob, but the recognition of your instinct to flee forced you to remain. Your hand dropped to your side. "But we have to keep in mind the fact that Sophie is just as fragile as any of them, right?"

"'Fragile'?" said Eric, chuckling. "Sophie?"

Your stomach tingled. "She's a kid. I realize she doesn't much look like one, but it's what she is."

"All right, all right. I was just joking around."

"But it's not a joke. If we treat her like she's something other than a kid, we'll be sending a harmful message. We're her teachers after all."

"He's right," said Tim.

Eric threw up his hands. "Jesus! I know he's right, but it's just us guys in here."

You fought the urge to back down. "We've got to be better men than that, right? While these kids are here, we're like caretakers."

"In loco parentis," said Tim.

You looked at him quizzically.

"It means 'in place of the parent,'" he said. "It's our responsibility, legally, to take on the functions and responsibilities of the parent when their child is in our care."

"Christ," grumbled Eric. "I know what it means."

"Well I didn't," you said. "Thank you, Tim. But it's more than that. It's our job to make sure they're safe and to help them finish a homework assignment or prepare for a test, but we have the opportunity, if we take it, to give more than that. And whatever that more is, I get the feeling that it's what really helps them in the end."

"We've promoted an idealist," said Eric, swiveling back to his desk.

Tim scratched his head. "We don't disagree with you, Josh. It's just that there's not always time for that. Right?"

"There is out there," you said, nodding toward the door that led to the study room.

"I've got to plan Haley Joel's chemistry unit," said Eric. "You should get back out there, Josh. Just make sure that before you bond or counsel or whatever it is you do, those kids have finished their algebra."

Tim stood up, stuck out an awkward hand, and you shook it. "Thanks for stepping up and helping us out." As you turned to leave, he patted your back. "You're gonna do a great job."

Considering the amount of time they'd been unsupervised, the study room was relatively quiet. Rafi gnawed away on ravaged pencil number two; the first one, its eraser severed by the same incisors that had depressed deep trenches along the length of its shaft, lay discarded by his notebook. A trio of new recruits, here to hone their college application essays, patiently did their homework and awaited their ten-to-fifteen minute windows of individual attention while Caspian and Adrienne huddled in a pocket of poorly-restrained giggles, defacing some kind of flier. Bent over her plate of fries, Sophie caught you out of the corner of her eye and gestured wildly. She pulled the vacant chair beside her back from the table and beckoned you to sit.

Soon the parents of all these kids would have to pay extra to get your attention. You wanted to feel okay about this, it wasn't as if the study room was pro bono work, but there was an honesty between these kids that you would miss—the solidarity derived from the public acknowledgment of the need for help. The Adriennes and Sophies of the world would never in a million years be friends at school and yet, under this roof, they were family.

You sat down next to Sophie and filched a French fry.

"Finally," she said.

"I need you to do something for me, Soph."

She raised a suspicious eyebrow. "Yeah?"

"Before we start whatever it is that's so urgent…"

She unleashed a torrent of words. "I have a huge essay due next week on *The Old Man and the Sea* and the outline is due tomorrow and I have no…"

"Hold it," you said. "We'll get to that. I just…" You leaned in conspiratorially and whispered. "I need you to help me get the word out about Adrienne's play. It opens tomorrow night and you wield a lot of influence in here. If you could just talk to a few people…"

Her eyes got wide. She swiveled in her seat and shouted, "Adrienne!"

Adrienne and Caspian looked up from their task, mouths agape.

"You bitch! I can't believe you weren't going to tell me that your show opens tomorrow!"

Adrienne's face turned pale and she tugged at her studded collar. "I was totally gonna to tell you, Sophie. I'm sorry. I just…"

Eric stuck his head out the office door. "What's going on out here?"

Sophie pointed at Adrienne. "Adrienne's play opens tomorrow night and she wasn't even going to tell us!"

"Look!" said Adrienne, producing the sheet of paper that she and Caspian had been hunched over. It said: *Forbidden Fruit,*

An Original One-Act. Beneath the title was the defaced picture of a square-jawed, high cheek-boned boy, who, at the impish hands of Adrienne and Caspian, had lost a few teeth, sprouted a pair of horns and acquired a thought bubble containing the words: "I am so like handsome."

Sophie looked perplexed. "Why did you mess up your own poster?"

"I was just making some improvements to his stupid face," said Adrienne.

"Girls," said Eric.

"Oh no!" Sophie jumped up, grabbed her plate of fries, and moved to Adrienne's table. "He rejected you?" She offered the fries to Adrienne, who quietly pushed the plate away. "I'm so sorry!" Caspian grabbed a handful and chomped away, eyes and lips glistening. "That guy's an idiot."

"I was stupid," said Adrienne. "I don't know what I was thinking."

Eric threw up his hands. "Am I completely invisible?" he said.

If you have to ask, you thought.

"I'll take care of it," you said.

"Good." He shook his head and closed the office door. You sat at the far end of the long table as Sophie, Caspian, and Hope—Caspian's older sister who had materialized out of thin air at the first hint of gossip—crowded around Adrienne like she was a wounded kitten. They held her arm, stroked her hair, injected their voices with cooing, soothing lilts and prodded for more information. You averted your eyes and scanned the bookshelf in an attempt to give them some semblance of privacy but the gesture went unnoticed. As the minutes elapsed, you wondered if they'd forgotten you were there, or if the whole thing was some kind of production intended to demonstrate to themselves, as well as any witnesses, just how adult their concerns had become.

"Hey everybody," Sophie suddenly announced to the room. "Please come see Adrienne in her play tomorrow night, even though the lead is a total douche bag."

The kids snickered.

"You must be freaking out!" said Caspian, holding Adrienne's hand.

"About the play?"

"I can't imagine having to perform with that guy after what he put you through."

Caspian's choice of words made you smile. From what you'd overheard, it sounded as though this guy's greatest offense had been having the gall to ask out another girl after calling Adrienne a couple of times for help with an English test.

"I probably would be freaking out if I thought about it like that," said Adrienne, "but it's not me on that stage."

The coterie mulled this one over, squinting and chewing lower lips. Adrienne elaborated.

"I mean that I'm whatever character I'm playing, you know? That's one of the reasons I love acting. It liberates me from my own little crises."

There was, amongst her listeners a not-so-subtle lifting of the eyebrows, as their expressions evolved from befuddlement to admiration.

Adrienne's gaze wandered to the ceiling, then back to her rapt audience. "And hey, if, for some reason, my feelings for him happen to surface while I'm up there, I'll use them. Like in method acting, when actors summon old wounds while they're on stage in order to embody the right emotions. But this will be even more legit because my emotions and the character's emotions will be in perfect alignment. The timing is actually super serendipitous."

The girls were silent for a few beats, each one staring at Adrienne as though they were either in awe of her or afraid that she might suddenly assume her natural, alien form and bite their heads off.

"Holy shit," said Sophie.

"Yeah," said Hope.

Caspian gripped Adrienne's arm. "That was like way super smart."

Adrienne blushed and bowed her head.

"Uhm, no offense to Josh," said Sophie. "But do you think you can you help me write my Hemingway essay?"

"Ewwh, no way," said Adrienne. "Hemingway was a total misogynist. He makes my skin crawl."

They laughed and Adrienne beamed. It was only when she caught your eye and smiled that you realized she'd been aware of your presence all along.

*

THAT NIGHT THE WEATHER turned. After work you walked along the edge of the park. The fog lay thickly upon the trees like a hangover. Beads of condensation plunged from leaves and splashed the dirt track with the solid thwack of summer-fattened insects colliding with lamp-lighted windows. Near the corner, where the track curved severely to the left, a woman sat rigidly on a concrete bench, bathing in the green glow of a traffic light. She had long dark hair and, even at a distance, an air of tragedy about her, as though her trials resided both in the present as well as the past, and the view from where she sat was a bleak expanse of more of the same. You stopped about fifty yards away and nudged an acorn back and forth with your shoe. Could it be her? It wasn't hard to imagine June haunting your neighborhood, waiting for a chance encounter to lead to one thing and then another.

You thought about Adrienne and about character—about the ways in which she'd recently grown, and the ways in which pretending to be a different person might have bolstered her sense of self. When the lights dimmed and the curtain fell, the actor shed her costume and changed back into her own clothes, mannerisms, speech patterns. There's knowledge to be gained in a return. Perhaps the person to which she returned was concrete in a way she never had been before. When an artist finishes a poem or a painting and they put it aside for a period of time, their return to the work accommodates a new perspective and clarifies what they were trying to express. A version of that is possible through acting. The character was her sculpture, poem or painting. Therefore, her return to Adrienne came with a heightened awareness of the ways in which she was different. By identifying who she was not, she could discover who she was.

For two weeks you'd stepped outside of a role you'd played for far too long. Now the question was, with your time with June ostensibly over, were you at peace with the person to which you'd returned? The answer was no. The person you were before her had always been searching for a June to care for. If you were going to change from that guy into the man that you wanted to be, the one you were in the process of defining right now, you would need to imagine something different. But imagination can be dangerous; it can limit you if you let it. Socrates said "the unexamined life is not worth living," but you had witnessed the other side to that coin. It was your friend Amare, paralyzed by the fear of relinquishing his imagination of himself, of allowing his head to be filled with *their* ideas about what he should want. You understood his fear. *They* can be very convincing. And once they've supplied you with the means to purchase those creature comforts that are so difficult to jettison, you've commenced an implacable march toward death.

The woman stood up from the bench and stretched her hands above her head. In the green glow of the traffic light it was impossible to tell, but her silhouette was a dead ringer. You could feel your pounding heart in your throat. All you needed to do was turn away, cross the street, and she would be eclipsed by apartment buildings.

Your phone rang and you quickly dug into your pocket to silence it but it was too late. The woman turned. She was too far and it was too dark to clearly make out her face. She might have been June. But there was no way to be certain without moving closer or calling out her name. For a few seconds, you stood there in fog-rendered anonymity. Finally, you summoned the person you were with Adrienne, stepped into his posture, his prudence, his confidence; you walked away, waiting at the curb for a few cars to sail by before crossing the road amongst the drift of dead leaves and energy bar wrappers. You fought the impulse to look back until just before you rounded the corner. The woman had vanished.

The apartment was empty. You switched on the living/ dining room lights and suddenly everything became clear. It was time to move. This home didn't belong to you anymore. You'd surrendered dominion. The couch now belonged to Amare, the floor to Bill, and invisible tracks laid by June's ceaseless pacing haunted all the spaces in between.

You ventured out to the balcony, the old refuge, and for whatever reason, the lone place that remained sovereign territory. Cigarette butts, survivors of the broom's bristles, wedged themselves against the doorframe. You gazed at them dolefully, mourning the loss of smoking the way you might a reliable companion who moved away. You were never going back. In the past, when you'd tried to quit, you fantasized about some minor tragedy or crisis that might give you an excuse to fail—being dumped by a girl, a false positive on a pregnancy test, getting fired from a job. In the fantasy, your transgression would be excused and you would be granted a finite window of guilt-free smoking because after all, a smoker was still a smoker when the chips were down. You recognized that, just as it was time to leave this apartment, it was time to leave the person who needed those toxic companions to feel secure. Let go the slouch in your posture, the mumble in your voice, the sweat on your brow. Let go the one who whispered "sleep" when it was time to wake and "panic" when it was time to sleep. Let go the phantom, haunting this balcony. Move on and encroach upon his territory no more.

Amare came home moments later and joined you on the couch.

"Hey," he said.

"Hey."

"I can't get over how weird it is to be the only pedestrian on a Thursday night in a big city."

"Yeah."

"I'm going to miss things about this place though."

"Yeah?"

Amare looked around the apartment and nodded.

"Well I'll sure miss you," you said. "I would have been seriously lost without you guys."

He chuckled. "That's a pretty generous perspective. You're a great friend, Josh. Far as I'm concerned, you're the best thing this city has going for it."

You lowered your head, nodded, took a deep, quiet breath and slowly exhaled. "Any word from Bill?"

"He's out getting drinks with that Sadie girl."

"Oh yeah?"

"Said it'd be a quick one. He's got the morning shift tomorrow."

"Our working man."

The intercom buzzed. You sprang from the couch, noting a faint but selfish hope that Bill's drink with Sadie was already over, and pushed the talk button.

"Hello?"

"Your male escort is here."

"All right," you said, "but you better be short, bald, and furry like in the picture. The last guy had a head of Samson hair and the body of an Olympic swimmer."

Bill laughed. "You won't be disappointed."

You pressed the buzzer and broke the seal on a bottle of twelve-year-old single malt scotch you'd sagely tucked away in the recesses of a cupboard.

"You've been holding out," said Amare. You grinned. "I don't blame you, dude. You don't break out the good stuff for couch-surfers until they're on their way out the door."

The three of you drank, watched Red Sox highlights, and avoided talking politics, opting instead to calculate Bill's chances of scoring with Sadie. You encouraged him to eschew the conventional don't-shit-where-you-eat wisdom and go for it, despite the fact that you could see yourself asking her out sometime soon if she didn't go for Bill.

Liberated from uncertainty, the conversation flowed like water down an unclogged drain. Absent was the outbreak of uncomfortable pauses that had infected breakfast at Loretta's, but discomfort was replaced by a tacit melancholy, the nostalgic laughter that accompanies the final days of summer. Back east, the leaves would have long since turned, but it took the approach of winter for the languid crawl of Los Angeles to acquiesce to the year's desire to wind down. It was just after midnight when you realized there was no milk in the fridge.

*

THE WIZARD'S SILVER HATCHBACK sat alone in the 7-Eleven parking lot, but it wasn't until you were abreast of it that you realized why it sagged so low to the ground. Like the solid iron core of the earth, the Wizard sat within. You crossed in front of the windshield and waved cautiously. He stared straight ahead, unblinking and pale. The hairs on your forearms and the back of your neck rose to attention and you moved quickly to the passenger door. You knocked on the window. Wearily, his head turned. A smile creased his waxen face.

"You all right, Ozzie?" you said through the closed window.

He nodded and gestured with his hand for you to open the door. You did so and a deluge of fast food wrappers and coffee cups spilled onto the ground.

"Damnation," he said. "Just toss them back inside."

"Don't worry about it. There's a trash can right here."

You gathered crumpled wax paper with bits of congealed cheese and ketchup-gone-brown, resisting the urge to flinch in revulsion.

"I hate to contaminate Habib's noble receptacles with my foul refuse."

You shoved handfuls of the garbage into the trash, got a tissue from your back pocket and wiped your soiled hands.

"Out, out vile spot," the Wizard murmured.

You mustered a hollow laugh.

"I'm sorry, Joshua. Care to sit with me a while?"

More garbage was packed solidly into the legroom between the seat and the floor. You'd have had to sit cross-legged.

"I'm just picking up a couple essentials," you said. "You want to come inside? Habib looks bored."

"I would like that very much, but I'm just now in the middle of catching my breath."

You frowned. "Oh."

"Don't look so concerned," he said, smiling thinly. "A mere bout of indigestion has left me a bit fatigued."

You laughed, relieved to not be burdened with a fresh, unexpected worry. "I'm gonna buy you something to help take care of your belly. Don't refuse. I owe you at least that much."

"As you wish."

"Any preferences?"

"I leave the decision to you, my friend." He winced and pressed his fist against the center of his chest.

"Ozzie? You sure you're okay?"

His face contorted with pain and turned scarlet.

"Ozzie!"

He let out a thunderous belch capable of penetrating the thickest of fog and guiding lost ships to shore.

"Excuse me," he said modestly, as if he had sneezed or done something equally prosaic.

You laughed. "Holy crap!"

He wiped his forehead with a checkered handkerchief. "One too many bacon-cheeseburger dogs."

You pressed your hand against your chest. "Jesus, Wizard. You scared me."

"To be honest, I scared me too."

"I'll be back in a sec. You sure you're all right?"

"Much better, my friend. Thank you."

You crossed the threshold and the electric doorbell chimed. Habib looked up from a crossword puzzle and smiled, his handsome face fresh and alert despite the late hour and longevity of his workday.

"I have meant to ask you how your shoulder is healing, Joshua. Is it much better now?"

"It is," you said, rubbing it gently. "I hardly even notice it." You snagged the last box of Honey Bunches of Oats from the shelf and put it on the counter.

"And your friend with the head injury. I haven't seen him for a few days. He is okay too? No headaches, nausea, confusion, fatigue?"

"Well, fatigue and nausea are sort of Bill's baseline, so that's kinda tough to say."

"Is this true?" said Habib, frowning in concern. "He should go right away to a doctor if he…"

"I'm kidding, Habib. It's a joke. Bill's fine."

You moved to the drink isle and contemplated the cheap beer, trying to remember which kinds Amare refused to drink on principle because of fascist CEOs and/or contributions to right wing political action committees.

"I was glad to hear that he found a job," said Habib.

You decided to splurge, tucked a sixer of Sierra Nevada under your arm, hefted a two-gallon jug of low fat milk, and placed the items on the counter beside your cereal.

"Yeah, Bill's all set up, but I'm afraid Amare's leaving us."

Habib stroked his mustache and nodded. "I do not believe that this city was the ideal place for him."

"I'm not sure it's the ideal place for anyone," you said.

Habib's brow furrowed.

"I'm not saying I'm leaving right away or anything, but it's starting to feel inevitable."

Habib scanned the milk.

"Maybe it's not the city at all," you said. "Maybe it's me." You dug your wallet out of your back pocket and rifled through your cash in search of a twenty. "I can't seem to figure out where I fit."

"I thought you said you were a teacher."

"I guess."

"Well are you or are you not?"

"Okay. I'm a teacher."

"Teachers are needed everywhere." He scanned the beer and typed your birth date into the register. "Everywhere a teacher goes, they transcend their environment. By helping students connect their small worlds to the larger one, teachers demonstrate how to think beyond the constraints of individual lives. If you are a teacher, you will have students wherever you go, and if you have students, wherever you go, you are home."

Habib put the scanner down, folded his arms across his chest and looked you dead in the eyes. Ashamed of your inexperience and uncertainty, you lowered your gaze to your tattered sneakers.

He cleared his throat. "May I say something presumptuous?"

"Of course."

He sat down on his stool. "To have an easy upbringing is a good thing, but it does not prepare one for life's more difficult decisions. You have kindness in your heart and an inquisitive nature, and that is most important. Go and share those qualities with your students, many of whom have not had to invent worries and manifest their own suffering because they are overwhelmed by the guilt of having been born into privilege and love."

You cleared your throat but found no words waiting to come out. You nodded.

"Good. One hundred dollars please."

You chuckled. "These microbrews sure are expensive."

"I'm kidding." He smiled. "It was my joke. Sixteen-seventy-four."

You looked down at the paltry items that sustained you. "Shit. I forgot to get Ozzie some Pepto." You turned to signal the Wizard, to assure him that you were looking after him. Even from a distance, through the glass doors and the loud advertisements alerting customers to specials on beer and soda, you could tell that something was wrong. You bolted outside and halted a few feet from the car, immobilized by the Wizard's impossibly blue eyes, wide-open to eternity, gazing beyond his car's streaked windshield as if attempting to take in the whole of the starless night.

*

SUMMER HAD ITS LAST gasp the day the Wizard was put in the ground. Trapped by the resurgent heat, a thin film of brown smog hung over the Valley. The funeral home was having trouble with their air-conditioning and the cloying stink of flowers lacquered the inside of your nostrils and sat heavily in your lungs. You imagined the Wizard soaking the inside of his silver and baby-blue casket with bucketloads of sweat, decorously mopping his brow with a handkerchief as he prepared to embark upon the ever after.

It was mercifully short service, with the pastor reciting a generic bit of scripture that could have applied to anyone. The three of you sat in humbled silence, you in a wrinkled grey suit you hadn't had the time or the skill to iron, Bill and Amare in borrowed button-down shirts and their darkest pairs of jeans. Habib and a elderly Black man with snow white hair and a burgundy Members Only jacket rounded out the mourners. No one spoke but the pastor. The entire service took fifteen minutes.

Afterwards, as you walked to your cars to drive to the cemetery, Habib pulled you aside.

"Josh, I must go back to work. Can you do something for me?"

"Of course."

You followed him to his silver station wagon, marveling at your easy rapport. You realized that, even as you were getting acquainted, you'd never anticipated a relationship with the Wizard or Habib outside of the context of the convenience store. The fact that you could suddenly see yourself being invited to Habib's house for dinner, or vice versa, excited you. This was something that, a few months ago, you could not have predicted. And that was a welcome sensation. It suggested you were doing something right.

Habib ducked inside the car, retrieved a plastic 7-Eleven bag and handed it to you.

"I do not know if this is appropriate, but I thought that if he…it would be a comfort to me to know that we are not sending our friend off empty handed."

You looked inside the bag and smiled.

He extended a hand and you shook it. "I will see you soon?"

"You're a prince, Habib."

He blushed. "Six months ago I could not have imagined that Ozzie's presence in my store would be something I would miss."

"I hear you."

You and Amare drove to the cemetery, Bill following behind in the Chevette. Amare's suitcase sat in the trunk of your car, packed for a one-way flight to New Jersey later that evening.

"Bill's cutting it awful close," you said. "Doesn't his shift start soon?"

Amare shrugged.

"You okay?"

"I'm fine. Ozzie's the one being buried."

"You want to talk about it?"

"Not especially."

You nodded and drove on.

Thankfully, the family plot, located on a rise in the Forest Lawn cemetery overlooking Burbank studios, was shaded. It was also, considering the fact that there were only three bodies interred there, quite spacious. Jaques Oswald Hinton, born on September 23rd, 1955, had died on September 23rd, 2003, just minutes into his forty-eighth birthday. He was laid to rest beside Bernard and Lucille Hinton, loving parents, dead fifteen and three years respectively. They had been old parents, born forty-four and fifty-two years before their son. Ozzie must have been a surprise, maybe even a miracle, coming along years after the couple had given up trying and resigned themselves to their childless lives. This seemed to fit. Ozzie'd had a certain quality—he'd been precious to somebody once. You couldn't help but imagine him taking care of his mother for those twelve years after his father had passed away. Maybe that was when he quit working, dropped out of society, began the overeating that accelerated his demise. Caring for the elderly can make a person exceptionally fearful of growing old, especially when faced with the prospect of doing it alone. Maybe he had lost the will to care for himself on the traffic-clogged freeways that led to his widowed mother.

More words were spoken but you didn't pay much attention. You kept a curious eye on your friends. You'd expected the kind of demonstrations of physical discomfort you get from children—the unbuttoning of collars, tugging at their bunched-up, tucked-in shirts, scratching and fidgeting. But they engaged in none of that. They stood there stoically and solemnly and you could see, in their composure, their fortitude and experience. You saw men acquainted with loss.

The casket was lowered into the ground. You, Bill, Amare, and the man in the Members Only jacket lined up on one side, the pastor and the gravediggers on the other. "Shy, quiet young man," said the stranger, which sounded natural enough coming from someone well over seventy, "but you catch him in the right mood, he'd just about talk your ear off." He watched the casket as though he were waiting for a light to change. "Didn't know he had friends."

"We weren't friends exactly," said Amare.

The man scrunched up his face, his lips pursed like a lumpy lemon rind.

"He was something of a local legend," you said.

A hoary left eyebrow climbed the man's forehead.

"He helped me out of a serious jam once."

"Good," the man said tersely, so everyone could hear the period. "Ozzie needed something to feel good about."

Amare winced but refrained from comment; as the gravediggers began to shovel dirt onto the casket, he wandered off a few paces and stood in the pounding sunlight. You removed the contents from the plastic bag that Habib had given you—a Lotto ticket and a bacon cheeseburger dog in a red and green cardboard container.

"Okay if I toss this stuff in there?"

The gravediggers looked at each other and shrugged.

"Do what you gotta do," one of them said.

The bacon-cheeseburger dog sprang from its container on impact as the Lottery ticket twirled and fluttered in blithe descent. It touched the surface of the casket face-up, it's hopeful numbers legible for a few fleeting seconds before being buried beneath a shovelful of uncompromising earth.

You and Bill wandered over to Amare.

Bill squinted into the yellow-brown sky as rivulets of sweat streamed down his forehead. "When my uncle died, only about a quarter of the family showed up for the funeral." He wiped his head and shook the sweat from his fingers. "He was a compulsive liar who everyone hated, but I don't think that they stayed away from the funeral because they hated him. I think sometimes people stay away from funerals because they're not ready not to hate."

"You think there's like a forgiveness ratio?" you said. "X years spent in the ground absolves you of Y years spent being a total dick?"

"That depends on the person, obviously," said Amare, loosening his tie and unbuttoning his collar.

"Ozzie was a saint," you said.

"You ever see him outside of 7-Eleven?" said Bill. "Maybe that place was some kind of self-imposed purgatory."

"Ozzie was a genius," said Amare. "We should all aspire to have his level of commitment."

Bill laughed. "Are you kidding me?"

"Do you realize how much discipline it takes to be as educated and intelligent as he was and live the life that he did? If more people had that kind of discipline, all our problems would be solved."

"You've lost me," you said.

"You guys want to go stand in the shade?" said Bill. "I could fill a kiddy pool with the sweat from my lower back."

"See what I mean?" said Amare. "Can't even stand in the sun for three minutes without running for cover."

"Try living in this pasty white skin for a day and see how you like it!"

"I'm just making a point," said Amare. "The Wizard was committed to an act. And that act made him a joke to others. It made him a subject of ridicule and derision, but he weathered their judgment like a fucking champion. He endured."

"What others are you talking about?" you said.

"I don't know. Everybody!" he shouted, flailing his arms around his head, indicting grass, trees, tombstones, clouds.

You paused for a few seconds and then spoke softly. "Ozzie was smart and he was educated. But you're acting like withdrawing from society took courage."

"Maybe it did," said Amare. "Maybe it took more courage than the alternative."

"Oh, that's horseshit," said Bill, walking off toward the shade and the steadily filling hole in the ground.

Amare wiped his forehead. "I think I'm done here."

"C'mon," you said. "Final respects and then we go."

The man in the Members Only jacket and the pastor were gone. You, Bill, and Amare sat in the shade of the eucalyptus and waited for the gravediggers to finish. When the job was done, you stood over the tightly packed earth, staring at it like it held the answer to a question that none of you had had the guts to ask.

Bill broke the silence. "The Wizard was the first stranger to talk to me after I moved here."

"Me too," said Amare.

"Me too," you said.

The boys looked at you like you'd just confessed to having sex with kitchen appliances. "Since I moved back anyway."

"Seriously?" said Amare.

"A few weeks ago. He made a comment about my hangover."

"But you moved back here from school like four years ago," said Bill.

You scratched your chin and gazed off into the smog as you considered this. "Yeah," you said. "A little over four years ago now. Fuck. I've been out of college longer than I was in it."

"That's crazy," said Amare.

"Time is speeding up," you said.

"Time is getting ahead of itself," said Bill.

Amare said, "I meant that it's crazy that it took four years for you to have a conversation with a stranger."

"That's this city, man." You chuckled. "Strangers don't pay you no mind. You don't keep reminding them, they'll forget you're here."

You dug a tissue out of your back pocket and mopped your brow. "When I went to June's mom's funeral, there were dozens of people there that June hadn't seen in years. Relatives that had stopped returning her mom's phone calls and whatnot. She, her mom, had been real secretive about her illness, so it wasn't like they'd known and done nothing to help her, but still, if June's sister hadn't gone through the Rolodex and called everyone, those people wouldn't have shown. Maybe June would never have seen them again. But she acted happy to see them, and when they said that they wanted to be there for her, she held their hands and smiled and thanked them. When no one ever called, she didn't say shit. I guess she wasn't surprised."

Bill exhaled loudly. "Thanks, Josh. I didn't think I could get any more depressed."

"An honest question," you said. "Would you rather have a few sincere mourners at your funeral, or legions of people, many of whom have only shown up out of sense of obligation or guilt or…I don't know…for the sake of appearances—to make it look like they gave a shit, like they weren't the self-involved pieces of shit they really are?"

"Funerals are for the living," said Amare. "I'll be dead so what should I care?"

"I just pray I outlive my mother," said Bill.

"Yeah?" you said.

"It's not like I'm looking forward to burying her," said Bill. "It's just that I don't want her at my funeral. I don't want my mom crying all over the people that knew me, telling them what a great son I was. I don't want all those people lying to her through their teeth and her getting solace from bullshit."

You laughed. "Jesus."

Amare chuckled. "Bill, you have a singular ability to find the absolute most depressing angle to a hypothetical question. You should do *that* for a living."

"That have health benefits?" said Bill.

Amare smiled. "Idiot."

"Asshole," said Bill.

"I need water," said Amare. "I'm gonna pass out if I don't get hydrated."

Bill clasped his hands at his chest. "Thank you."

"One more minute," you said.

Amare glanced at you and nodded. Bill ground his shoe in the yellow grass.

"It feels important to just…" You didn't finish your thought. Didn't have to.

The sun moved across the sky and light seeped through the tree shade, pooling on Ozzie's grave. The three of you baked in it for a couple of minutes before someone sighed, another turned and gradually, the ineluctable tug of time and duty drew you back to your respective rides.

*

SOMETIMES THE ONLY WAY to leap forward is to first fall back. It's the correction of the original motion, the reactionary thrust that catapults you past that place where philosophy or inspiration petered out and left you standing on well-worn territory with nothing but another false epiphany and less time left to figure it all out than you had going in. You recognized something of yourself, something of every friend you'd ever had, in the Wizard's drive to obliterate his mortal flesh. It was easy to admit this to yourself. Surprisingly, the revelation brought you some peace. Because there was beauty in the man, in his slovenliness, in the way he made no attempt to conceal his demons. And while the feeling you had felt toward him might not be so accurately characterized as admiration, that was definitely part of the mixed bag of emotions that churned in your gut as you sat in a gray metal folding chair, in a high school theater, and Adrienne materialized on stage in a shaft of golden light, wearing a melancholic expression at once very Adrienne and very different.

Some actors can captivate an audience without uttering a single line; their expressions and gestures reveal the inner life of the character and evoke an emotional response that stems from the recognition of something true. The dialogue was sophomoric, full of sentimentality, clichés, and poor imitations of the way adults speak. In addition to this, Adrienne's co-star, the handsome young man who had been the object of such controversy at The Homework Club, found a way to inject a pregnant pause into nearly every line, so that the action came to a screeching halt every time he opened his mouth. None of that detracted from the sincerity and grace of Adrienne's performance, or the pride you took in her success. As the drama unfolded, you couldn't help but recall the first time the Wizard spoke to you. He had called you and your profession "noble." You'd peered at him through hungover, sleep-encrusted eyes, and, despite your condition, he bolstered you with his esteem. He made you believe, in that moment, a moment in which you felt nothing but nausea and self-loathing, that there was an apparent goodness in you, and later that day, you'd carried that feeling into your work with Adrienne. You had been a better, more confident teacher. For that trick alone, the man deserved his moniker.

Soon enough, the one-act was complete and the curtain fell. You and Harrison lingered on the periphery of the mob that swarmed Adrienne, patiently waiting your turn. The Homework Club had come out en masse, Sophie and Caspian each bringing a few friends with them. And then there was the family. You had never actually seen Adrienne's mom or dad, but they were easy to identify, clinging to their new partners as they fussed over their daughter and surreptitiously eyeballed one another's dates, inventorying all observable flaws.

You waited, expecting Adrienne to be Adrienne—deliver a bashful nod in your direction before spending an obligatory moment by your side where she might hang her head and humbly accept whatever praise you lavished upon her. So it took you by surprise when she saw you and her eyes went full-moon wide and she pushed her way through the crowd and unabashedly threw her arms around your neck. She released you and you stepped back, stunned, glowing like that robust spotlight had been trained directly on you.

"What did you think?" she said, her sparkling eyes locked with yours.

"You were *amazing*," you said.

"They dropped a sound cue and for a second I was like, totally ready to panic, like, what do I do if the phone doesn't ring, you know? But then I remembered what you said and I just repeated the line and they got it. Did you notice?"

"I did not," you said, lying through your teeth. "You were too smooth."

She laughed. "Nah. Of course you noticed it, but that's cool, I don't mind. I expect you to notice things that other people don't."

You turned to Harrison to tell him that it wasn't usually like this, that he shouldn't go making any assumptions about your skill or ability, that it was highly unusual for your students to smother you with credit and hugs, but before you could put this into words, or even into some kind of facial expression that might convey roughly the same thing, Sophie sauntered up beside Adrienne and slipped her arm through her elbow.

"Doesn't our Adrienne look hot?" she said, fussing with Adrienne's hair.

"Stop it, Sophie," Adrienne said, smiling hugely.

"Don't get me wrong, babe, dying your hair green was like, totally badass, but this reddish brown color is *way* sexier. You look like that girl in *Titanic.*" Sophie turned nonchalantly back to you and said, "Who's your friend, Josh?"

"Harrison," you said, "Meet Adrienne and Sophie. Two of my star pupils."

Harrison extended his hand. "You were great."

"Oh," said Adrienne. She took his hand and pumped it once very formally, nodding at him as she did it. "Thank you, sir." She smiled at Sophie like this was the funniest thing that had happened to her all night.

Harrison stuck his hands deep in his pockets. "Interesting show."

Adrienne looked back toward the stage, as though the ghost of her performance lingered there. "The script still needs some work."

"No!" said Harrison. "It was good. The whole fluidity of sexuality thing..."

Sophie's eyes widened at the mere utterance of the word "sex." She swept her hair behind her shoulder and stuck out her chest. Seized by a sudden coughing fit, Harrison buried his face in the crook of his elbow.

"Great stuff," he said in between smoker's hacks. "Very timely."

"What did you think about the sexuality, Josh?" said Sophie.

You chuckled. "To be honest, I was more interested in the actors than the ideas." You nodded at Adrienne. "She's right about the script, but it didn't detract from her performance." You pointed at Adrienne. "You were brilliant."

"Aw shucks, Teach."

"Now go back to your adoring friends. I'll see you two Monday."

Adrienne gifted you a smile that you immediately framed in your mind's gallery of Images to Preserve. "See you Monday," she said.

You and Harrison wordlessly navigated the crowd and emerged onto the black asphalt of the parking lot. Beside it were half a dozen basketball hoops.

"I wish we had a ball," said Harrison.

You grinned, retrieved your basketball from the trunk of your car and gave it a few dribbles.

"Could use a little air," you said.

You whipped a pass over to Harrison and he air-balled a three-pointer.

"They get heavy when they're flat," you said.

"Shut up," he said, running after it.

He jogged back to the free throw line, took a few dribbles, bent his knees, and knocked one down. You caught it before it hit the ground and sent it back to his chest. This time he dribbled it through his legs, stepped back a couple feet and his jump shot caught nothing but net.

"Jumper looks good," you said.

He tossed you the ball and you walked out to the free throw line. You dribbled a couple times, bent your knees, and released it. It landed softly on the front of the rim, rolled around for a second, and fell through.

"You always had a soft touch, Teach." He sailed the ball back at you.

You knocked down another free throw and wandered out to the left wing. "I had all the confidence in the world when I was a kid." You banked one in, jogged to the corner, caught the pass from Harrison and shot a deep jumper that caused a slight stab of pain in your shoulder. The ball rimmed out. You pinned your arm across your chest, pushed on your elbow and held the stretch. "When I got older, like by the time I was thirteen or fourteen, I lost confidence, turned into a classic practice shooter. My shot abandoned me during games."

Harrison dribbled the ball out to the three-point line and sank it. He said, "I've gotta say, this low self-esteem shit is getting old." You grabbed the rebound and passed him the ball. "I'm tired of you thinking that you're not something that you are." He knocked down another three. "Like with those girls in there, the way that you handled them, what you mean to them." You zipped a pass into his waiting hands. He launched again but came up short. The ball careened off the front of the rim and back out to him. "You're an important person in their lives."

"I know."

"Do you?" He dribbled the ball and stared at you.

"Yeah."

"Good. So just own that and stop worrying so fucking much." He launched another three from the same spot and came up short again. "Goddammit."

You grabbed the rebound and fired a pass into his waiting hands. "Knock it down, shooter," you said. He jumped, followed through and the ball rattled home. "There you go, baby."

"Yeah, yeah," he said. "Get out there. I'll rebound for a minute."

You jogged out to the top of the key and massaged your shoulder. "You okay?" he said. "Something hurt?"

"I'm good." You held up your hands. Harrison fed you a pass and you dribbled a few times.

"Don't think," he said.

You bent your knees and sank a set shot. The discomfort in your shoulder was negligible. He rifled it back to your waiting hands. "You're a shooter," he said. "Shoot." You sank a jumper and moved back to the corner. As he fed you the ball, your mind went blank and your muscles warmed, until soon you felt no pain at all, only the sweet satisfaction of the ball finding the bottom of the net.

Acknowledgments

SPECIAL THANKS TO TYSON Cornell, Julia Callahan, and all the folks at Rare Bird Books for your talent, energy, humor, and kindness. Above all, thank you for your belief in this book, and for never once suggesting that I ditch the second-person point of view.

Thank you to K.M. Soehnlein, Malena Watrous, Howie Krakow, and Joshua Mohr for going above and beyond, and to all my professors at USF for your wisdom and encouragement.

To my peer editors, Calder Lorenz, Charlie Mandell, and Jenny Skogen, thank you for your blood, sweat, and tears. Or, at least your lower-back pain. I am forever grateful for your smart eyes.

Thank you to Bacchanal—to Nick Van Brunt, Jesse Krakow, and Jon Damon—without whose delight in the silly and the absurd, my adolescent heavy-handedness might have become a lifelong affliction.

Thank you to Josh Smart, Abi Hassen, and Will Gruen, for the inspiration; to Adam Machado for the pep talks; and to Alex Maslansky, whose intolerance for ego and bullshit sentimentality has positively influenced my creative efforts since I was fourteen years old. The fact that you helped put this book into the world is all the affirmation I'll ever need.

I'm a lucky guy. This is not something of which I ever lose sight. Without the luck of having been born into the unyielding love and support of my parents George and Kathy Wyner, and my brother Nick, this book would be no more than a lonely kernel, rattling inside my brain, forever waiting to burst open.

And there are no humans with whom I'd rather celebrate this book's publication than the ones who are there for me everyday, in all possible ways, the loves of my life: my wife Nora—without whom I would be a little more than a puddle, dirty and cold, shivering in the abject solitude of a pothole—my stepdaughter Ciel and my son Dashiell.